Radcliffe

By Madeleine D'Este

First published by Deadset Press in 2023.

Cover design Copyright © Austin P. Sheehan.

Edited by Austin P. Sheehan.

isbn: 978-0-6450228-8-9

Acknowledgement of Country:

In the spirit of reconciliation, Deadset Press acknowledges the Traditional Custodians of country throughout Australia and their connections to land, sea and community. We pay our respect to their Elders past and present and extend that respect to all Aboriginal and Torres Strait Islander peoples today.

Contents

Chapter One

Day One

'Death is coming,' the Voice said and Tamsin trudged on. Up and down the unfamiliar sun-bleached streets she went, lost yet unconcerned. Could a person be truly lost if she didn't know her final destination?

Sweat slithered down the channel of Tamsin's spine as the relentless morning sun blasted onto a cluster of dog turds on the footpath. The shopping strip with nail salons, kebab houses and real estate agencies had dwindled into tyre shops, shabby offices and warehouses with broken windows. Occasional tumbledown workers cottages were sandwiched in-between.

'Warm,' the Voice said and Tamsin turned left, stumbling down another semi-industrial street. It was quiet in an unnerving way. Harsh February light reflected off windows and windscreens into Tamsin's eyes, and blinded, she tripped on a shifting plate of concrete.

'Warmer.' This voice was the authoritative one. Loud and strong, a headmistress or a general. A tone accustomed to being obeyed. Yet, the Voice sounded exactly like Tamsin's own.

'Cold,' the Voice snapped. Tamsin lifted her head and whirled around. A neglected office with mail piled up like autumn leaves. A taxi company. More sun and no trees. Where?

'Death is coming. Warmer,' it teased.

"What do you mean?" she said aloud and crossed to the other side of the street without looking. A car horn blared and someone swore.

A dull jab of pain accompanied every step, her pointy shoes rubbing the corn on her left little toe. If she'd known she was going to be wandering the streets today, she would have worn more comfortable shoes. But that was not the way the Voice worked.

'Warmer. Warmer.'

Here? She passed dented cars outside an accident repair mechanics, queued up like patients in a waiting room. A seedy-looking man, coveralls rolled down to his waist revealing hairy back and shoulders, smoked under the shade of an awning. Tamsin averted her eyes and picked up her pace.

'Boiling.'

She jerked to a stop and looked up. A house. The name *Radcliffe* engraved on a tarnished brass plate by the door.

'Death is coming.'

Three storeys high with peeling beige paint and weeds sprouting from the gutters, the ramshackle house sat between a panel beaters and an abandoned building site. A hand-written sign sat in the grimy ground floor window:

Flat for Rent. Enquire Within.
Women Only.

Before she knew what she was doing, Tamsin rapped on the blackened brass knocker.

Above her head, a sash window groaned open and a woman yelled. "Coming."

Tamsin stood sweating on the doorstep until an elfin crone opened the door. White hair in a neat bun on top of her head, wrinkled eyes lined with black kohl and a gnarled walking stick in her hand. "Yes," she said with a plummy voice, her snub nose in the air.

"The flat." Tamsin plastered on her best smile. "Is it still available?"

"For the right woman . . . yes." The old lady sized her up and down and Tamsin smoothed back her sweat-dampened hair. At close to six foot with a physique suited to rugby, Tamsin loomed over most people, but she was a giantess next to the slight white-haired woman.

"I'm Bunty Hetherington," the woman said and graciously held out an age-spotted hand with long red nails. Tamsin shook Bunty's hand, but in her eagerness, her grip was like iron. With a cringe, she let go of the older woman's fingers and flashed an apologetic smile.

3

With an elegant flourish, her stick thumping on the worn linoleum, Bunty ushered Tamsin into a dim windowless hallway with high ceilings. The olive-green walls ended with a staircase covered in crimson and gold threadbare carpet.

Bunty gestured to her right where a brass number one hung on a scratched antique timber door. "Radcliffe has five flats. Two on this floor—"

"And only women live here?" This simple fact intrigued Tamsin. It must be why the Voice led her to the building.

On the left, a tarnished gilt-framed mirror sat above a side table piled with letters and junk-mail, and a large box lay on the floor addressed to LG McGovern in Flat 3.

"Oh yes. It's much better that way. Men are too much trouble. But you are a woman of"—she gave Tamsin another penetrating once-over—"experience. You understand."

Tamsin wilted under Bunty's appraisal. She was only thirty-eight years old, but the toll of the last year had fast-tracked her face into middle-age.

"But where was I? Yes, there are two flats on this floor, two on the next floor and I live on the top floor with my grand-daughter."

"Up all those stairs?"

"They're no bother. The stairs and I are old friends." Bunty produced a jangling ring of keys from her pocket. "Here we are."

"Do you own the building?"

The old woman cackled. "Do you think I would let this old dear get so run-down if I owned it? The owners have entrusted me with a master key." She unlocked the door and, with a heave of her cane, forced the sticky door open.

Like the foyer, the room had lofty ceilings and drab grey-green walls. Tamsin wrinkled her nose against the stale and damp air. Grubby net curtains covered the only window onto the street and dust lay in clumps along the skirting boards.

'Boiling,' the Voice said. Tamsin clapped a hand over her ear. Even though she was the only one who could hear it, she couldn't risk the sound of the Voice leaking out.

"This is the lounge obviously," Bunty said. The dark floorboards creaked under Tamsin's weight as she followed the old woman through the empty apartment. Tamsin rubbed her chin. Here? The Voice wanted her to come here? Just walking through this shabby flat made her whole body heavy and dismal.

"Through there is a small kitchen and a bathroom. And a bedroom. All very basic. There's a back door too which leads out to a side alley running alongside the building. Although I'd keep it locked if I was you. Some strange characters about. Sorry, I didn't catch your name?"

"Tamsin," she murmured as she scoured the room, looking for something, anything, which would explain why the Voice led her here. She had to trust the Voice, but all she saw was a one-bedroom flat in desperate need of a scrub down and a coat of paint. Her thoughts hazy, she pinched the bridge of her nose. What on earth was she doing here?

"When can I move in?" she blurted before she had a chance to stop herself.

Bunty blinked. "Don't you want to look at the kitchen? And the bathroom? It's a bit poky and to be honest, there's a touch of mould, but it has a bath."

Tamsin crossed the room and stuck her head through one doorway then another. "It's fine. It's perfect. I'm looking for somewhere quiet."

The older woman cocked her head.

Tamsin babbled on. "I don't need much space. Can I move in straight away? Do you need references?"

"You haven't even asked about the rent?"

"I'm sure it's reasonable." Tamsin forced a smile.

"Cheap, yes, it's cheap. Of course it's cheap. And you don't need references." Bunty squinted at her. "I won't ask your story, Tamsin. We all have our sordid little pasts. There are far too many reasons why a woman like you might end up at a place like this. But I am a good judge of character and you strike me as a woman who pays her rent on time."

She wrenched two keys from the ring and handed them over. "Five hundred per month. We send our cheques each month to a lawyer's office. I'll bring down their business card later. Welcome to Radcliffe, my dear. I hope you'll be happy here."

"Thank you." Tamsin weighed the copper keys in her hand, her cheeks flushing with pleasure although she still didn't know why she was here. She already rented a townhouse in the suburbs.

'Death is coming,' the Voice whispered as if to remind her.

Tamsin sucked in a deep and sweet breath. This was why she was here. To help. To stop death from coming. The only question was—for who?

Chapter Two

Day Four

Three days later, Tamsin was staring at her boxes stacked against the dingy grey-green walls. The sweaty removalists had left only minutes earlier, after shunting some boxes, a couch and a spare bed from her real house across town in the fierce morning heat. She'd left her car behind with the majority of her belongings, and hitched a lift in the truck cabin with the two men. One, too old to be lifting furniture, reeked of last night's beer, and the other, a silent teenager. The stinky man prattled on at Tamsin the entire way, yet didn't ask her the one question she expected—why was she moving from a tidy modern house in Heidelberg to this dump? Like therapists and cleaners, removalists must see some strange messy things, and learn to be discreet. She was glad he didn't ask, she hadn't even justified the move to herself. There was a reason—some grand but mysterious plan for why she'd been drawn here—and for the moment, that was enough.

Eventually someone would ask, and she'd have to explain. Last year, when the Voice first appeared, she'd tried to tell her younger sister Abby after one too many bottles of Prosecco. Her friends on the forums had warned her, but Tamsin thought she knew better. She was wrong. Abby didn't react to her life-changing news quite the way she'd hoped. Then there was the incident with the client in her office. The last twelve months had taught Tamsin to be prepared. And it was often better to lie.

Footsteps thumped across the ceiling above her. Her upstairs neighbour. It was at least fifteen years since she'd last lived in an apartment, and now she was back surrounded by the intimate sounds of faceless strangers.

Her phone pinged from her handbag. As she checked the text, a customer service survey from the removals company, she noticed it was three o'clock.

Throwing her hand bag over her shoulder, she rushed into the kitchen, double-checked she'd locked the backdoor and grabbed a plastic bag off the counter. She yanked her sticky front door shut and headed up the ratty-carpeted stairs.

On the first landing, a cobweb covered window overlooked the street. There were two doors on the right, Flat 3 directly above her own—the source of the earlier footsteps—and Flat 4 was further down a narrow corridor beside the stairs.

After one more flight of steps, Tamsin arrived at the top, panting. How did the octogenarian Bunty manage these stairs every day? Tamsin calmed her breath and dabbed her sweaty face with a tissue before knocking politely on the door to Flat 5.

"Hello?"

"Come on in," Bunty called and Tamsin stepped inside a high-ceilinged room which stretched the entire width of the building. Curtainless windows faced north and south. The peeling wallpaper was busy, with enormous shiny white flowers and green palm leaves, a style of decor Tamsin hadn't seen since her suburban childhood. A fan revolved in the corner, blowing air over Bunty and a plump, dark-haired woman.

Bunty waved from her place on the worn green velvet settee. "Welcome."

"Sorry I'm late. I lost track of time," Tamsin said, then turned to the other woman who sat opposite Bunty in a matching armchair. "Hello, I'm Tamsin."

"Nice to meet you," the dark-haired woman said with a hesitant smile. Dressed in billowing black, her brown eyes were as fidgety as a mouse.

"Defne is from Flat Four," Bunty said. "Take a seat, my dear."

Tamsin slid into the closest vacant armchair, broken springs sagging under her weight. The three women sat in a triangle around a low battered coffee table, decked out with a floral tea-set and doilies. Tamsin clutched the grey plastic bag to her chest and wished she'd gone to more trouble.

Bunty lifted the bone-china teapot. "Milk? Sugar?"

"Please. White with one."

With surgeon steady hands, Bunty prepared the tea, then added a sugar lump with silver tongs.

Tamsin placed her handbag gingerly onto the floor and rustled the plastic bag. "It's only cheese and crackers, I'm afraid. Smoked cheddar. Sorry, I should have baked something."

"It's perfect. Something savoury. I always invite Defne because she bakes the most delicious cakes," Bunty said as she handed over the tea cup and saucer. The delicacy of the china made Tamsin nervous. "You must try her revani. Is that how you say it?"

"You're too kind." Defne blushed and leaned forward to cut Tamsin a diamond-shaped slice of cake. While her attention was elsewhere, Tamsin scrutinised Defne's wide face. Was Defne the one? Was death coming for her? She studied her neighbour and waited for the warning signs, the tell-tale ringing in her ears, the nausea. But there was nothing. The Voice was silent.

"Cecily?" Bunty called out across the lounge room.

A willowy young woman in tiny shorts appeared from deeper within the flat. She leaned against the doorway with a half-eaten piece of toast in her hand. "You called, Grandmama?"

"Bring out a plate and the cheese board for our guests, please?"

"Anything for smoked cheddar," Cecily said with a grin and twirled back out of sight.

11

Tamsin followed her with her eyes. Perhaps death was coming for her? Her heart slumped inside her chest as she imagined the death of someone so young.

"My granddaughter. She's staying with me while she studies psychology at Melbourne University," Bunty said. "Do you work?"

"Yes, in tax . . ."

"Tax. Oh." Bunty blinked. "Well, I guess that's necessary."

"I'm on a sabbatical at the moment." Tamsin pulled at her collar. Thankfully Defne interrupted her, offering her a plate.

"Grandma here was a ballerina." Cecily reappeared with a wooden board and another floral plate. "If you can't tell. I keep telling her, she really should change her hair."

The old woman patted her tight white bun and thrust her chin higher into the air.

"Wow," Tamsin said. "I've never met a ballerina before."

"It was forever ago," Bunty said, with a toss of her head. "Now I'm merely a teacher."

"She has the best stories," Cecily stage-whispered. "Tell them the one about Swan Lake and the flood."

"Another time." Bunty swatted at her granddaughter with a playful paw. "Radcliffe has always been a haven for the Muse. Defne here is not only a fabulous cook, she's also a photographer."

12

"Although I'm not very good." Defne wrung her hands, twisting the three chunky silver rings on her left. "In fact, I should be"—she shot up out of her armchair.

"Don't be silly," Bunty scolded. "Stay."

Defne dropped back down onto the cushions like a rock into a pond, and scrubbed her hands in her lap again.

Picking up her fork, Tamsin cut the tiniest piece of cake. It was all part of the ridiculous game women played around food. She slid the demure morsel between her lips. The moist nutty cake was sweet and tart with an exotic hint of rose water.

"Delicious," Tamsin said and lunged for another forkful, this time a little larger.

"An old family recipe," Defne replied and for a brief moment, the frightened rabbit look left her face.

"Egyptian?" Tamsin asked, taking in Defne's dark hair and eyes.

"Turkish."

Tasmin nodded. "Have you been at Radcliffe long?" she said. Although the question she most wanted to ask was why Defne was living here, the same question Bunty refused to ask her on the day they met. There had to be a reason why she was living in such a tatty apartment building. She imagined it wouldn't be a happy one.

"A few years now," Defne muttered and then flew up to her feet. "I really should be getting back to my work. I don't want to miss the afternoon light." She yanked her handbag up off the floor and scurried out the door in a flurry of black fabric.

Tamsin grimaced while Defne's sandals slapped across the linoleum and down the stairs. "Was it something I said?"

"She's even stranger than usual today." The coltish Cecily flopped down onto the couch beside her grandmother. Tamsin searched for a resemblance between the two women but found none. Bunty was pale and blue-eyed while her granddaughter had a golden complexion with sea-green eyes.

"The torture of an artist, Cecie," Bunty said. "I don't expect you to understand."

"Oh I understand," Cecily replied. "I just haven't quite worked out where she sits on the ratings. Bipolar? Or perhaps post traumatic stress?"

Bunty rolled her eyes affectionately. "One of Cecie's little games. She diagnoses everyone."

Tamsin swallowed, now self conscious of her every word and gesture, and changed the subject. "Tell me about the other women who live here. I heard the lady above me walking around this morning."

"Ah, the mysterious Gail," Cecily said and sliced another thin sliver of cheese. "Apparently she's a disgraced diplomat, hiding away."

"Who told you that silly story?" Bunty tutted.

14

"Or in witness protection."

"Does that even exist in Australia?" Tamsin frowned. If this were true, Gail could be the one in danger.

"Agoraphobic, I reckon," Cecily said. "She gets everything delivered."

"Gail is LG McGovern?" Tamsin asked.

"Another fan?" Bunty exclaimed. "Isn't she wonderful?"

Tamsin grimaced. "Sorry. Is she famous?"

"You're not some crazed groupie, then?" Cecily arched an eyebrow.

"No."

"Then how did you know her name?" Cecily quizzed, leaning forward on her elbows.

"I saw a box in the hallway," Tamsin said, her cheeks flushing with heat. "And you said she had everything delivered."

"Oh," huffed Buffy. "Well you must read her. She writes the most terrific historical fiction with a bit of romance." She pointed to the overflowing bookshelves in the far corner of the room, next to a table with a sewing machine. This time Tamsin saw the cracked plaster, the pools of damp like pustules on the ceiling and the cobweb strings on the architraves. "You're a reader, of course?"

"Oh yes," Tamsin said. Although before the Voice came, she'd never had time to read. At the end of a day of spreadsheets, public transport and housework, she was too exhausted to do anything but stare at a flickering screen. Since her break from work, she'd rekindled her old childhood friendship with books. Non-fiction mainly, the answers Tamsin needed about the Voice, and her new direction in life, couldn't be found in the crime dramas and reality shows on TV. "So Defne is in number four, and Gail in number three, who lives in Flat Two?"

Bunty pursed her lips.

"You'll meet Riko soon," Cecily said. "Or her music, more likely . . ."

Tamsin waited for Cecily's diagnosis of her next-door neighbour, but instead the fledgling psychologist reached for more cheese.

"She never gets up before midday," Bunty said. "Please let me know if the noise bothers you."

"She works nights?"

"You could say that," Bunty sniffed.

"You don't know it for certain, Grandma." Cecily turned to Tamsin. "She's a DJ or a musician or something."

"Terrible racket whatever you call it," Bunty said with a sigh. "Usually I'm an excellent judge of character. I guess we all make mistakes."

"It sounds like you've been living here for a while, Bunty?"

"As Cecie said I was a dancer. I travelled with troupes across the country and abroad. Europe, London, America. I was so lucky." Her eyes glazed over. "But I injured my knee in the early seventies. So long ago now. Even then I was already over the hill in dancer years, and as poor as a church mouse. I needed some cheap digs and I landed here, and for one reason or another, this is where I've stayed."

"Do you know who owns the building?"

"I'm not completely sure these days. The rent goes to a lawyer's office in the city. Originally a man named Gideon Inchcombe owned it. He died soon after I moved here and then I believe Radcliffe was placed in a trust. If there are any maintenance problems, we have a little man who comes around . . ." Bunty's voice wavered. She let out a whimper and swiped at her forehead.

"Are you okay?" Tamsin leaned forward.

Cecily jumped up from the couch. "Time for your meds, Grandma," she said and disappeared into the depths of the flat.

Bunty shaded her eyes with her age-worn hand. "I'm sorry, Jane."

"It's Tamsin." She winced, then bit her lip, regretting the correction.

"Of course, silly me." The old woman grabbed her walking stick and, with a ballerina's grace, glided up to standing. "It must be this atrocious heat."

"Is there anything I can do?"

"It's nothing a little lie down won't solve. Please stay and have another slice of cake. And take one of Gail's books."

"Thank you for inviting . . ." Tamsin spluttered but Bunty was already half-way across the room and then disappeared through a doorway.

Alone and feeling awkward, Tamsin sat in the lounge room as the fan whirred in the background and a door closed somewhere deeper inside the flat. Should she leave? She shifted her weight in the armchair. But this was the perfect chance to interrogate Cecily further.

Tamsin finished her now lukewarm tea, and after a minute or two, Cecily wafted back into the lounge.

"Will your Grandma be okay?"

She asked the question out of sheer politeness, because somehow Tamsin knew Bunty wasn't the reason she'd been drawn to Radcliffe. It was sad to say but at her age, Bunty's days were numbered. The death Tamsin was seeking felt more torrid, muddled, and thorny.

"She forgets she's not young anymore," Cecily said, helping herself to another cracker with cheese.

"She's lucky to have you looking after her."

"Ha. Bunty doesn't need me. I'm the one who needs the cheap rent."

Tamsin chewed her lip and nodded, flicking away an intrusive thought about her own finances, now faced with two rents to pay.

Cecily turned her green eyes to Tamsin, making her fidget in her seat. They may not share colouring but Cecily had inherited her grandmother's weighty stare. "Now, what's your story? Let me guess . . ."

Heat flashed up Tamsin's neck. She was supposed to be the one asking the questions. "You know, the usual."

"Divorce?"

Tamsin nodded. "Last year."

The truth was she'd never been married. However-from that moment on-as far as the residents of Radcliffe were concerned, she was a divorcee. She'd have to be careful and keep track of all her untruths. Perhaps she needed a list.

". . . and you mentioned a break from work. Sorry if this is a bit personal, but can I ask? Is it stress leave?"

Tamsin's mouth dropped open. Had she ever been as confident as Cecily? Let alone during her early twenties.

Without waiting for a response, Cecily continued. "Are you seeing someone? Professionally? A counsellor?"

Tamsin gripped the delicate teacup and produced a rictus grin. When she first told her sister about the Voice, Abby had pulled a few strings and arranged an appointment with a psychiatrist. There'd been two awkward sessions with the mellifluous Dr

Prakash, mainly to appease Abby. Of course, it was a complete waste of time, the doctor didn't understand.

"I'm doing a unit on counselling this semester. So if you need anyone to talk to. Completely confidential, of course." Cecily leaned forward, her face glowing. "Any time. Just ask."

"Thank you." Tamsin blinked, her tone flat and formal. "I'll bear it in mind. I should be going. All that unpacking to do."

"Thanks for coming up. Grandma loves meeting new people. I hope you like living here. Despite everything . . ."

Before Tamsin could ask her to elaborate, Cecily leaped up and left the room, returning with an empty plastic container, and, after a detour to the book shelves, a book - 'Druid's Kiss' by LG McGovern.

Tamsin grabbed the empty ochre-coloured plate. "I'll take Defne's plate back to her."

Cecily gave a half-shrug as she filled the container with what was left of the revani.

Tamsin was soon back downstairs pacing around her new shabby apartment. She couldn't even call it shabby chic.

While debating with herself about whether to eat the rest of Defne's cake, she was met with a new, unexpected sound. The thump thump thump of electronic dance music echoed through the lounge room wall. Her notorious neighbour Riko must be awake. Tamsin groaned and slumped down on her old familiar couch.

She chewed on her bottom lip, replaying every moment of the afternoon tea, every word and gesture of her new neighbours, scouring for clues to why the Voice had been so insistent she came to Radcliffe. So far, she had no idea. Her belly fluttered. It had only been a few hours though. There was still plenty of time.

"I won't let you down," she said to the empty room.

#

After unpacking her meagre boxes and eating all of Defne's semolina cake, Tamsin lay on her old couch and opened up Druid's Kiss. Before long, her eyelids sagged and the words floated on the page.

A loud knock at the door eventually disturbed her catnap, waking her with a jolt. The book tumbled off her lap and landed on the floorboards with a thump, and she jumped a second time.

She blinked away the haze of sleep. Where was she? Drab walls. Hint of mould. General cloud of dismalness. That's right. Radcliffe. The death house. And yet the Voice which insisted she come here, which dragged her up and down the streets of North Melbourne on foot during a heatwave, was absent. The strange music from next door had stopped too.

Another knock sounded. It wasn't her door but the front door of the building. She sighed. This was going to be one of the drawbacks of living in Flat 1. She groaned up off the couch and slipped on her thongs.

It was six steps from her flat to the main front door. As she opened it, a wave of searing heat blew inside, and two stony-faced constables in uniform were standing on the step. Tamsin suppressed a gasp. Had death come already and she'd missed it?

"Gail Peterson?" the tall freckled-nosed female cop said.

"Erm . . . no."

Peterson? Wasn't Gail's name McGovern? Then again LG McGovern must be one of those writer's nom de plumes. She'd Google her later.

"Is Ms Peterson here?"

"I'm not sure. I only moved in today," Tamsin said. "Sorry, I mean I haven't met her yet."

The woman continued with an expressionless tone. "Do you at least know where we can find Flat number three?"

"Oh yes, I do know that," Tamsin gushed and stepped aside to let them in. "Upstairs."

The female cop and her associate, a young man with sticky-out ears, stomped across the foyer and up the stairs in their heavy black boots. Tamsin slunk back into her own apartment and waited behind the closed door. She stared up at the high ceiling and followed their footsteps above. A crack in the plaster over the door caught her eye. On closer inspection, it was a word that had been clumsily engraved into the wall like graffiti on a school desk. She squinted and stretched up on tip-toes but still couldn't read it.

A firm knock rapped up above her head. Tamsin flinched. Then she waited for footsteps, for Gail to answer the door, but there was nothing. After a few seconds of silence, there were mumbling voices echoing down the stairs. Tamsin tilted her head.

"Ms Peterson. Victoria Police," the female Constable called out, loud enough to leak through the ceiling. "Can you please open the door?"

The flat above was still, not even a single curious footstep crept towards the front door. Maybe she was out and Cecily was wrong about the agoraphobia?

The police knocked again. "Ms Peterson. Please open the door."

After another minute of quiet, the police boots clumped down the stairs and towards the front door.

Disappointed, Tamsin turned back to the word carved in the ceiling above the door. She gripped onto the peeling door trim and reached up as high as she could. Did it say *COMING*? She couldn't be sure. Maybe it was time for an eye test.

A sharp rap sounded on her door. Tamsin flinched, then waited a beat before opening up the door.

"Oh hello again." She tried to sound casual. "Any luck?"

The bland-faced female cop handed her a business card. "If you see Ms Peterson, can you give this to her?"

Tamsin took the card with two fingers and held it away from her body. "I've never met her though."

"When you do meet her"—the woman spoke in a slow and deliberate way as though Tamsin was a child—"ask her to call us. It's important."

"You might be better leaving something under her door or with the lady who lives on—"

"Already done. Have a good afternoon," the cop said and walked away.

Tamsin closed her door and went back to the mysterious word. Peering up again, it was only a crack in the drab grey-green plaster. Either it was a trick of the light, or she did need glasses. Her shoulders slumped and she glanced up, wishing she could see up through the dirty white ceiling and into the flat above. Why did the police want to speak to Gail? Had someone died? Death was coming after all. Or was it something mundane like parking fines? While she speculated, footsteps thudded across her ceiling, then the door of Flat 3 opened.

"Bastards!" a woman yelled.

The door slammed shut again.

#

About an hour later, Tamsin grabbed Defne's clean plate off her dish rack and headed upstairs to find out more about the fidgety photographer.

The air was stagnant on the first floor. A few degrees warmer than her flat but milder than the sweltering outside. Old brick walls like Radcliffe's provided protection against a hot spell for a few days. But if a cool change didn't arrive soon, the building would become a furnace, with no respite inside or out.

Tamsin rapped gently on Flat 4's door.

The door flew open. Defne's eyes were electric. Her dark hair was in a messy pile on top of her head, stray strands snaking out in all directions. "Yes?" she blinked.

Tamsin recoiled then held the plate out like an offering. "Sorry to bother you. You left this at Bunty's."

Defne took the plate from her and stared at it as though she'd never seen it before.

"I'm Tamsin." She faked a broad smile. "We met this afternoon?"

"Oh yes, of course . . . Tamsin," Defne mumbled. "Sorry. Sometimes it takes me a few minutes to come back to reality."

"Oh no." Tamsin winced. "Did I disturb you?"

"No. Your timing is good. I got a couple of half-decent shots." She exhaled and smoothed back her wayward hair. "I feel almost human again."

25

Tamsin gave an awkward nod, the false smile stuck firm on her lips.

Defne went on. "That's why I rushed off from Bunty's earlier, I just had to get back down here to finish my pieces. You know, I can see the image I want to capture clearly in my mind but I just can't get it." She grimaced and clenched her fist. "It drives me bonkers."

Art was an alien world to Tamsin but the description reminded her of life with the Voice. When she needed it most, like now, it was nowhere to be heard. Even when she did hear it, it was so vague that she was left puzzling for days with no idea what to do. Yet she was certain the messages were important. She'd been chosen as a vessel and she had to help.

"Come in." She waved Tamsin inside with a generous smile, her black kaftan wafting around her curvy frame.

Tamsin chewed on her lip. Was this the same nervy woman from afternoon tea?

The layout of the dark and stuffy room was a mirror image of Tamsin's own flat, the thick curtains along the northern side were drawn shut. Lights on tripods, electrical cords and rigging cluttered the room. One bright spotlight focused on a trestle table in the centre of the otherwise shadowy space, radiating heat like a pocket-sized sun. On top of the table sat three tea-cups, a bushel of lemons both whole and halved, a coil of barbed wire and a

26

large dissected brown rat, its pink innards spooling out onto a doily. Tamsin stifled a gasp. Death had already arrived at Defne's.

"Still lifes are my passion," Defne said, ignoring the dead rodent on the table and walking straight towards the kitchen. "I'm trying to capture the prison of female stereotypes. Bit ironic, really."

Tamsin nodded but she had no idea what Defne meant. Why would anyone choose to photograph dead rats in their lounge room? She wanted to know more but assumed she wouldn't understand the explanation, and instead followed Defne into the kitchen, averting her eyes from the slimy intestines and furry carcass.

The kitchen was the same as her own but Defne had somehow squeezed a table for two into the tight space. Shelving ran above the table with rows of spice jars and green seedlings in small pots. She rinsed off the plate then gestured for Tamsin to sit down on a low stool at the table and Tamsin fumbled down onto the seat. Her bottom sagged over the sides and her knees were crammed up by her armpits.

"I love chilled lemongrass tea on days like this." Defne yanked open the fridge, pulling out a jug and a sprig of white grapes.

"I've never tried lemongrass tea before but anything cold sounds lovely. I'm not a fan of this weather."

"I like it. I think I'm part reptile. Although when winter rolls around, I'm a whingeing pain in the arse." Defne poured out two large tumblers and placed the grapes on the ochre plate.

The iced tea was zingy and refreshing. "I might have a new favourite drink," Tamsin remarked.

Defne popped a grape into her mouth and they fell into silence. Tamsin's mind buzzed like an angry fly. The whole point of her visit was to learn more about Defne, to find out if she was the one death was coming for, but now she was lost for words. How did you get people to confide in you? Numbers were always Tamsin's strength, not people.

"Did you hear the police earlier?" she asked.

"Police?" Defne's eyes grew wary again. She fiddled with the silver rings on her hand.

"A few hours ago. They were asking for Gail."

"Interesting . . ."

Tamsin paused and waited for Defne to tell her more, but the reclusive photographer filled her mouth up with grapes instead.

"Has this happened before?" Tamsin prodded. "The police coming to see her, I mean."

Defne shrugged. "I wouldn't know."

Tamsin leaned forward. "How long have you been neighbours?"

"She's been here the whole time. Three. No, four years."

"Cecily thinks she's agoraphobic."

"I've only seen her a handful of times and we've never spoken. Apart from her writing, I don't know anything else about her. Except for what I've heard from the others. Really though, what would a nuclear physicist be doing living here?"

"I thought she was a writer?"

"Like I said, I wouldn't know." She popped another grape in her mouth.

This conversation was going nowhere. It was time Tamsin tried a different tack. She raked her fingers through her hair and heaved a dramatic sigh. "I haven't lived on my own before, you know. This is the first time."

Defne tilted her head. "Really?"

"Do you like living here?" Tamsin continued her pretence. "On your own?"

"I love it." Defne placed a hand against her heart.

"That's good to know. I didn't have much choice. Take my advice, never marry a lawyer." She sighed again.

Defne leaned forward and nodded. "My bastard husband kicked me out too. He hooked up with a new woman, and suddenly I was the homeless one."

"How awful," Tamsin said but she tingled at the first scrap of new information. "Any kids?"

"No. Unfortunately, not. He's got one with her now though. I guess it must have been my fault. Anyway, he shoved me aside for her and I ended up here. But don't worry, Tamsin"—she gripped hold of Tamsin's hand across the table—"it was the best thing that ever happened to me. And you'll feel the same. Given time."

She crushed Tamsin's fingers and her face shone like a religious zealot's. "You'll experience the true spirit of freedom. How wonderful life can be when you are yourself. With no one else to interfere."

Tamsin nodded, mainly to encourage Defne to let go of her hand.

"I'm so glad you moved here," Defne mused and released her grasp. "Do you believe in fate? I think we were destined to meet. I hope we can be friends."

"Me too," Tamsin said and slipped her hand underneath the table, rubbing it in relief.

"The others here. They are all . . . a bit . . . strange."

"In what way?" Tamsin raised an eyebrow.

"You'll understand in time. It's so nice to have someone I can rely on here in the house. You're so stable . . . and normal."

Tamsin cleared her throat. "I'm nothing special. Just a divorced tax accountant with a few money problems."

"See! Normal."

Tamsin forced out a laugh. If only Defne knew the real reason she was here.

#

On the first night in her new bedroom, Tamsin lay wide awake in her old bed. Naked and sweating under a thin sheet, she pined for her home air-conditioning. Could she sneak back to Heidelberg for a proper night's sleep? Or would death come for one of her neighbours while she was out? And would she regret her selfish decision forever?

Aside from the occasional eerie creak and groan in the walls, Radcliffe was quiet. It had been three days now since the Voice had led her here, without another whisper. The Voice had always been as fickle as a Melbourne spring day, but had never sent her on a mission across town before. And now, had left her here with nothing. Had it abandoned her completely? Left her all alone to solve this for herself? Death is coming. But for who?

Footsteps stomped overhead and she traced their path with her eyes. A door slammed and someone clomped down the stairs. Tamsin leaped out of bed without turning on the light. In the unfamiliar room, she tripped and tumbled to the ground.

"Bloody hell," she grumbled and grabbed at her shin, and as she cursed, the front door of the building closed. Her shoulders slumped.

Throwing on a nightie, she yanked the sheet from her bed and moved to the couch, closer to the door. She didn't want to miss another chance to meet Gail.

After dozing off, she was woken by the creak of the front door closing again.

Wasting no time, Tamsin scrambled to her feet and wrenched open her flat door. A young Eurasian woman with damp shoulder-length hair stood in the shadowy foyer, dressed in a striped t-shirt, knee-length denim shorts and trainers. She blinked at Tamsin from behind her round framed glasses, and without a word, continued walking.

"Gail?" Tamsin sputtered. "I've been hoping to meet you."

The woman stopped and turned, a backpack slung over her shoulder. She grinned at Tamsin. "It didn't take you long."

"Sorry?"

"Radcliffe's favourite game. Catching Gail. I heard she's allergic to sunlight. Like a vampire." The woman snarled and bared her teeth. "I'm Riko from next door."

Tamsin's heart lifted. The infamous Riko. Should she invite her inside? Or would that be odd? It was one o'clock in the morning.

"With the music?" Tamsin said, licking her lips.

"I didn't know anyone had moved in. Flat One has been empty for a long time."

"But it's so cheap and central . . ."

Riko shrugged. "It's a weird building full of weird women. Anyway, I'll wear my headphones from now on."

Tamsin stood in the doorway in her nightie as her neighbour walked down the hall. That was Riko? She appeared nice enough—nothing like the degenerate Bunty had described. Tamsin closed her door and the shower started to run on the other side of the wall.

#

The yellow glow of street lights pressed against the thin bedroom curtains, and outside somewhere a man laughed, a dirty cackle that bounced off the bitumen and houses, but Tamsin thought only of Radcliffe.

Her new neighbours' faces flicked through her mind like a slideshow. Five women. Five possible victims. Who would die if Tamsin wasn't here to save them?

Her closest neighbour Riko was fresh in her mind. She was definitely stand-offish but Tamsin would be wary too if she'd been accosted by an enthusiastic stranger in the middle of the night. Cecily mentioned DJing, and nightclubs meant one thing, drugs. Overdoses. Car crashes. Tamsin recalled a story from uni about a girl run over by a garbage truck after stumbling out of a club at dawn. She pictured the vulnerable young Riko wandering alone down dark empty streets. Perhaps she needed to persuade Riko to stay home more. Then there was the mystery of why Bunty disliked Riko so much.

Next was Defne. Excellent cake-maker, divorcee and temperamental photographer, she'd only met her twice and had seen three different sides to her. What Defne would she get next time? Her creepy art could be a clue. Maybe there was an innocent explanation for the rat? Nostalgia for high school science experiments? Or could it be revenge, and the rat's original owner was coming for her? Tamsin shook her head to stop the compounding ridiculous thoughts. After a rocky start and one or two lies, at least Defne was keen to be her friend. Maybe a little too keen. With a few more coffee catch-ups, Tamsin was sure she'd know everything there was to know about Defne, including the story behind the dissected rat.

Moving onto Cecily. Young, pretty and effortlessly confident, although somewhat blunt in her diagnoses, and filled with the arrogant certainty of youth. Her relationship with Bunty was a joy to behold. Tamsin's own maternal grandmother had been a cold woman with stiff permed hair who smelled of wood polish and expected Tamsin to sit in the corner and stay quiet and clean, which she did. For most of her life.

A life cut short at Cecily's age would be a tragedy, but no one was immune. Was there another reason why she was staying at Radcliffe with her grandmother? Was she hiding from someone?

A jealous angry ex-boyfriend? The newspapers reported on jilted men killing their partners every day. Perhaps she should take up Cecily's offer of counselling and somehow get her to do all the talking. Tamsin cringed. But what psychological pigeonhole would Cecily put her in? And what would happen if she uncovered Tamsin's real reason for being here?

Then there was Bunty, the matriarch of the house, with her graceful gestures, sudden headaches and colourful tales of the stage. In her heart, Tamsin felt Bunty was not the reason why she was here. If only Tamsin could be so sure about anything else at Radcliffe. She rolled the thought around her mouth like a wine connoisseur. The mysterious death was more raw and unexpected, and this sense, this shape, this taste of death was something brand new for Tamsin. Her friends from the forums were right, she was growing into her gift like a child with a new pair of shoes.

And last was the elusive Gail. Every story she heard about the woman in Flat 3 was wilder than the last. Disgraced diplomat, witness protection, nuclear physicist, vampire. If any of the tales of her past were even vaguely true, there were plenty of opportunities for death. After her first full day in Radcliffe, Tamsin was no closer to the facts about Gail. Not even her real name. And why had the police been knocking on her door?

Five women and death was coming for one of them. So many possibilities, so many chances for death to sneak in. She couldn't be everywhere at once. And yet Tamsin was certain she'd soon discover who death was coming for. The Voice had chosen her to help. It must have faith in her.

"Death is coming," she whispered to the whole house and all her neighbours tucked up in their beds. "But so am I."

Chapter Three

Day Five

Tamsin was buttering toast at the kitchen counter when a mild ringing in her ears surged into a deafening static, engulfing her brain with white noise. She clutched at her head. The knife fell from her hand. A hot streak of bile burned up her throat.

Knowing the routine, she dropped her hands and grabbed the edge of the bench. The first time it happened she'd been waiting on Platform 2 at the underground Flagstaff Station, squeezed among the after work crowd. The ear-splitting hiss and nausea turned her solid legs weak and knocked her to the ground. She panicked, fearing it was a stroke, until from nowhere the Voice spoke to her. Despite her Godless upbringing, her first thoughts were of a demon. Or mental illness. This time however, she smiled.

The roar faded to a tinny hum, Tamsin wiped her forehead and waited for the message. She knew the Voice wouldn't forsake her. She had to be patient.

'Death is coming,' the Voice whispered. Her own voice, yet ethereal and bordering on seductive, in a way most unlike her. It filled her head, its words crowding out everything else.

"I remember," she said. "But I need more help. Who?"

Replying was pointless, the Voice never answered her questions. This was a one-sided conversation, a monologue of vague hints and instructions which she was compelled to follow.

'Screaming.'

"Screaming?" she repeated.

Tamsin rushed to the fridge and pulled her notepad from under a bag of carrots in the vegetable crisper. A hiding place she'd seen once in a crime drama and never forgotten. She grabbed her handbag and rummaged inside but couldn't find a pen.

'The screaming,' the Voice said again.

Shaking her handbag half a dozen times, Tamsin found a chewed pen in the depths and scribbled the word *screaming* on an empty page.

"Who?" Tamsin asked.

'Death is coming.'

Then, like turning off the television, the Voice was gone, Tamsin's head was free, and all she could hear was the coffee pot bubbling over on the stove.

\#

After a quick shower and sweating all over again, Tamsin was on the lumpy couch trying to decipher the Voice's message. Her phone rang and her heart clattered. It was her sister Abby. She rolled her eyes and let it ring.

"Coward," she muttered to herself and answered. "Hey."

"Where are you?"

"What do you mean?" she said, trying to sound casual.

"Where are you? It's an easy question to answer, Tam. And don't lie and say you're at home. Because you're not. I've been round three times since last night. Your car is in the driveway but you're not there. I came this close to calling the cops."

"I'm fine. You don't need to worry about me."

"I do when you do shit like this. Tell me where you are."

"Calm down."

"Don't tell me to calm down! Where the hell are you?"

Tamsin pulled the phone from her ear, her finger hovering over the red telephone symbol. Abby knew she was alive now, maybe she'd leave her alone. But this was her sister, the girl who applied to twenty different universities for three years running until she got a place at a top tier school to study law. Tamsin lied instead.

"I decided to get away. Take a break like we talked about."

"So where are you then?"

"A hotel in the city."

"What? Why? I thought you wanted to go down to the coast?"

"Too hot. There's a nice pool here."

Her sister grumbled and ground her teeth. "You still sound weird," she said. "Have you been hearing those voices again?"

"I've been reading this interesting book," Tamsin said. ". . . by the pool. You might like it. In the past, people assumed their own thoughts were the word of God. You know 'God told me to do it', rather than I decided to. It's only recently that we've begun to associate the sound of the voice in our heads with our own thoughts."

"Fascinating. Who's the author?"

"Erm," Tamsin said. "Some PhD. I can't remember."

"And you didn't answer the question."

"Do you hear your own thoughts in your head? Like a voice?"

"Sure but—" Abby replied.

"But what?"

"You know what you're hearing is different." Abby calmed and slowed her voice. Tamsin pictured her sister clenching her fists as she struggled to stay patient. "It's not the voice of God. You're not some Chosen One. It's an illness."

Tamsin's cheeks burned. How could her sister, wrapped up in her narrow world of corporate ladder climbing, children's private schools and renovations, possibly understand? There were hundreds of books and websites written by experts, explaining how the voices came from angels. Plus entire online communities of men and women just like her—people who knew the Voice was a gift not a curse—and assured her that she was not alone. The

Voice was a messenger, a harbinger of warnings. She refused to feel ashamed. She wasn't sick, she was Joan of Arc.

"I'm worried about you," Abby continued. "When are you coming home? Do you need me to come and get you?"

"No, trust me I'm fine."

"You said that last time and look what happened."

Tamsin swallowed hard. "This is different."

"Are you sure?" Abby sighed. "You know you scared me, Tam."

"I know. How many times can I say I'm sorry?"

"Don't apologise, just come home."

"In a few days."

"I'm not the only one who's worried about you. Have you spoken to Hilary? She called me the other day."

Tamsin frowned. "How did she find you?"

Hilary was Tamsin's manager at Austin & Chow Advisory, the accountancy firm where she worked. Where was this new concern coming from? Hilary hadn't cared a jot about her in the ten years they'd worked together. Life was all income tax, trial balances and bottles of Grange on corporate credit cards for Hilary. And it had been six months since the incident at the client meeting.

"I'll call her tomorrow," Tamsin said, although she'd wiped her manager's number the day she walked out of Austin & Chow.

"And Dr Prakash?"

"I've got an appointment with her on Thursday."

"You better not be lying to me."

This last statement was in fact true. The follow-up appointment had been booked a month ago, although Tamsin had no plans of turning up. There was no point, a doctor like that—her office wall lined with certificates from stuffy sandstone universities—would never understand the Voice. No one 'normal' could. This was the problem, but it was their problem, not Tamsin's.

"Call her office if you don't believe me."

Her sister grumbled. "I don't like this."

"It's okay, Ab. I'll be back in a few days. We'll go round to Tempest & Grape and I'll tell you all about it."

She sighed. "If you're not back by Sunday, I'm calling the cops."

"Alright. I'll see you then."

She ended the call and flopped down onto the couch, scraping her fingers against her scalp. What if Sunday was too soon? If Abby called the police, how long would it take them to find her? She frowned. Could they hunt her down using her phone? She swiped in and double checked all the privacy settings. Then she remembered there was no formal record of her at Radcliffe. She smirked and threw down her phone again. She'd call her sister on Monday, this should buy her a few more days. It should be all over by then and she'd be back in her air-conditioned comfort in Heidelberg.

Her mouth tacky with thirst, Tamsin heaved herself up off the couch and headed for the kitchen. As she reached into the cupboard for a glass, she glimpsed something in the sink and reeled back in horror. The glass slipped from her hand and smashed onto the floor. Inside her sink, curled-up, was a large dead rat.

#

In the side alley alongside the building, Tamsin lifted the wheelie bin lid. A wave of hot garbage singed up the insides of her nostrils as she dumped the dead rat inside. She was heading back into the courtyard, and coughing away the stench, when Cecily, dressed in tiny shorts and thongs, emerged from the ramshackle weatherboard laundry in the corner where an ancient washing machine lived. A basket of wet laundry in her arms, the long legged girl headed for the centre of the concrete courtyard where an empty Hills hoist stood like an iron tree.

Tamsin waved hello as she passed a cobweb covered barbecue and a weatherbeaten picnic table. "Does this building have a pest problem?"

"Spiders totally." Cecily shuddered. "Why?"

"I just found a massive dead rat in my kitchen sink."

"Ew." Cecily screwed up her pretty face. "What did you do with it?"

Tamsin pointed towards the bins.

"I'll ask Grandma to call the odd-job man. Emphasis on the odd."

The Voice had said nothing about a rat. Screaming yes, but nothing about rodents.

Tamsin chewed her lip as she glanced up to Defne's window on the first floor, the only other place in Radcliffe where she had seen a rat. "How much do you know about . . ." Tamsin lowered her voice. While Defne's windows were closed, their words might ricochet off the concrete and brick, straight into Defne's ears. ". . . about Defne?"

Cecily's eyes gleamed. "Do you think it was her?"

Tamsin opened her mouth, then decided not to mention the rat in Defne's photograph. It could be a coincidence. The rat in her sink had been in one piece, with all its intestines tucked up neat inside. Perhaps her rat had died a natural death, wandering into her flat in a desperate search for water.

"No," she said after a beat of hesitation.

"She's a bit of a strange cat. Though not as jumpy as she used to be. She can almost sit still long enough to have a conversation these days. Almost."

"She is changeable, isn't she?" Tamsin said.

"People are messy. That's why I find them so interesting." Cecily stopped and tapped her finger onto her lips. "Hmm . . . no one has lived in Flat One for ages. An empty flat is a perfect home for rats."

"I did hear scratching last night."

Cecily gave a dismissive wave. "That's just Radcliffe. You'll get used to it."

Tamsin stared up at the looming red-brick building, its windows like half-lidded bleary eyes.

"Interesting," Cecily continued. "Who could be responsible for your little present? If we're excluding natural causes." She raised an eyebrow. "Have you met Gail?"

"Not yet."

"Even after her visit from the cops?"

Tamsin frowned. "How did you know about that?"

"I saw them leaving." She gave an innocent half-shrug. "And when I went upstairs, I saw their card on her doormat and put two and two together. Did they tell you anything?"

"I was home the whole time," Tamsin said. "I didn't hear you come in."

Cecily did a little pirouette on her tiptoes, clasping the washing basket against her chest. "Perhaps I have the dancer's genes."

"Why would Gail plant the rat?"

"Maybe it's a warning. She's very private."

Tamsin picked at her fingernails. A warning? She hadn't done anything wrong. She was here to help.

A sash window opened above their heads with a groan.

"Cecie . . ." Bunty's white head appeared from the top floor window. "Antiques Roadshow is about to start!"

"I'll be up in a minute," she called back.

"Hello there, Sandra," Bunty said with a wave.

"It's Tamsin, Grandma." Cecily rolled her eyes at Tamsin.

"Oops, of course. Too many names over the years. Come join us if you like, Tamsin."

Tamsin shifted her weight from one foot to the other. Should she go back to the flat, and wait for another clue from the Voice instead? Before she could respond, Cecily shouted back on her behalf. "She'll be up with me in a minute. We have a mystery to solve."

"Perfect."

The window closed with a thump.

"It's our little evening ritual," Cecily said as she hoisted a white sheet onto the washing line. "Six thirty on the dot."

"Hasn't she heard of streaming?"

Cecily shrugged. "Hand me a peg."

Tamsin chewed her lip. Radcliffe was like an old fashioned island. Modern conveniences like streaming services would be out of place in the old house. She passed Cecily a pink plastic peg.

\#

A few minutes later, Tamsin and Cecily arrived upstairs. Posh English accents blared from the television and in the corner, the pedestal fan was blasting at full power.

"You've already missed the beginning," Bunty said as Cecily flopped onto the green velvet couch beside her.

Tamsin perched herself on the edge of an armchair, conscious of the slick of sweat covering every inch of her skin, praying that the fan would point her way.

"Coins. How boring," Bunty scoffed at the screen and turned the volume down. "So, what's this mystery?"

Cecily leaned forward with sparkling eyes. "Tamsin found an enormous dead rat in her kitchen sink."

"How disgusting!" Bunty said, curiosity rippling over her face. "How big was it?"

Tamsin held out her hands. "Almost filled the whole thing. Horrible yellow teeth. And long claws."

"Did it stink?" Cecily asked.

"Not really." Tamsin furrowed her brow. "Not like rotten flesh or anything. It was vaguely familiar. Like ammonia?"

"Revolting." Bunty shuddered. "And rather odd. We've never had a problem with rodents here before. Spiders, yes . . . cockroaches here and there but no rats. I'll get Philip in tomorrow. Don't leave any dirty dishes in the sink overnight is my advice."

"I reckon someone put it there," Cecily said.

"Deliberately?" Bunty squinted.

"Maybe it was a stranger?" Tamsin added. "I could have left my back door unlocked?"

Bunty nodded. "There are some weirdos around."

"My money is on Gail," Cecily said.

"Don't be silly, Cecie." Bunty tutted. "She's harmless. A trifle strange but harmless. I can't believe someone who writes such good stories would do something like that. And why Tamsin?"

"You don't think good artists can be bad people? Come on, Grandma. You know better than that."

"Queenie O'Hannigan!" Bunty snorted. "Impeccable dancer but what a piece of work. Slashed everyone's pointe shoe ribbons before the opening night of Coppelia because she didn't get the lead. And she got away with it. Scot-free. Nasty little minx. Never mind, she'd be dead by now. They all are."

"Gail has secrets . . ."

"I've told you the story about her marriage to a Mafia boss is absolute nonsense," Bunty said.

"When was the last time the police knocked on your door looking for you?"

"It happens." Bunty shrugged. "We can all be in the wrong place, wrong time. Could be something as innocent as a parking ticket. It doesn't mean she's a wanted woman."

"That's what I thought too," Tamsin jumped in. "But she was home the whole time. I heard her moving around after they left."

"Maybe she didn't want to be disturbed. She might have been in the middle of writing a particularly racy scene. I do love those bits." A salacious smile spread across Bunty's face.

"Grandma!"

Tamsin chuckled to herself.

"There is . . ." Bunty traced a finger over her bottom lip. ". . . another potential suspect . . ."

"Defne?" Tamsin exclaimed before she could catch herself.

"Defne?" Bunty blinked. "Have you two fallen out? I thought you were getting along famously? Visiting each other's flats like old pals?"

Tamsin tugged at her dress collar. That her comings and goings were being noted and discussed made her want to pack her bags and run back to her anonymous townhouse in the suburbs. Was anything secret in Radcliffe?

Bunty didn't wait for a response. "A rat in the sink." She rubbed her chin. "Very gory. It has to be Riko."

Cecily rolled her eyes. "Grandma."

"This is exactly the type of evil I was telling you about, and it's not the first time here in Radcliffe. Not everyone who's lived here has had good intentions."

"Don't go on about all that again," Cecily said. "You'll give yourself another headache." She turned to Tamsin. "Grandma's recovering from a run of bad health."

Bunty narrowed her eyes. "Apparently I'm so fragile I need to stop teaching."

"Just a little break." Cecily patted her grandmother's arm. Bunty shook her hand away.

"What do you mean by . . . evil?" Tamsin asked.

Cecily scowled at her but Tamsin pretended not to see.

"I have a feeling about people," Bunty said. "The house doesn't like her."

"Grandma." Cecily sighed. "How many times have we talked about this?"

"Don't be a fool, darling. This house knows more than you and I will ever know, the old dear. She is warning me about her. I should get her evicted. I must write to the lawyers."

"Maybe the house put the rat in Tamsin's sink," Cecily said in a deadpan voice.

"She would never do that!" Bunty exclaimed. "She likes Tamsin, although she doesn't understand why she's here."

Cecily shrugged at Tamsin. She smiled back weakly in reply.

The house wasn't the only one.

Chapter Four

Day Six

With her arms loaded with groceries, Tamsin stumbled back to Radcliffe under the scalding sun. As the footpath cooked the soles of her sandals, she fantasised about a wintry dip in the freezing waters of Bass Strait. While Tamsin was struggling through the building's front door, sweat pooling under her bra, a harrowing scream erupted from Flat 2.

Death was here.

She dumped her green shopping bags and raced across the foyer.

"Riko! Riko?"

She tried the handle. But it was locked.

"Are you alright? Riko?"

She thumped on the door, her knees shaking, the horrible screeching continuing, Riko's weird music in the background.

"Why didn't you warn me!" She was talking to the Voice but as usual, the Voice didn't reply. Picturing Riko with a knife jutting out of her ribs, splayed on the floor in a puddle of blood, she knocked again.

Tamsin fumbled inside her handbag for her phone. She emptied it on the floor and frantically sifted through the mess.

Then the scream stopped dead, replaced by a brittle silence. The quiet was more frightening than the cries.

Tamsin froze, fresh sweat beading her upper lip. Was she too late? Under her sunglasses case and a packet of tissues, she spied her phone and grabbed it. Then the music and the shrieking started all over again.

"I'm calling the police." Tamsin kicked at the door while her fingers floundered, dialling Triple 0. "Hang on, Riko."

The call connected after a few rings. "Hello? Hello!" she shouted.

"Fire, ambulance or police?"

"Police! Someone's being attacked. I can hear them screaming. Hurry."

"Where's your emergency?"

"It's a building called Radcliffe—"

The door flung open. Screeches burst out from the darkened flat. Tamsin stumbled back and dropped the phone from her ear, breath catching in her throat. She'd only been thinking of Riko, she hadn't even considered her attacker.

Riko emerged, barefoot in t-shirt and jean shorts with a cigarette in her mouth, and not a drop of blood to be seen. "Too loud?"

Tamsin wilted against the staircase and clutched at her chest. "You gave me a heart attack."

"Hello? Hello? Are you there?" Emergency Services were still on the phone in her hand. "What's the address?"

"Sorry," Tamsin replied. "False alarm."

Riko chuckled as Tamsin hung up. "Were you calling the cops? Now that's a first. I'll turn it down." Riko headed back inside her dark flat.

"I thought you were being murdered," Tamsin cried.

Riko stopped as another wave of shrieking and music squeezed past her. She took another puff of her cigarette. "I guess that does sound pretty fucked up." Her mouth curled into a crooked grin as she shrugged and turned away.

Tamsin's mouth hung open, her heart thundering. She scooped the mess on the floor back into her handbag, and then sighed before turning back to collect her shopping. Her apples had tumbled out, scattering across the dusty foyer floor. She bent to pick them up and noticed Riko had left her door ajar, and her music was leaking out into the hallway.

She left the apples and poked her head inside.

The blinds were closed and the only source of light was a series of computer monitors on the far wall. Riko was silhouetted against the screens as she tapped on a keyboard and stopped the strange music.

The sudden silence was heavy and uneasy. Tamsin scrambled for something to say. Music had to be her way in.

"Was that one of your songs?" she said, her voice louder than she expected.

"Fuck!" Riko jumped, her hand flying to her chest.

"Sorry to barge in on you. I'm just curious," Tamsin said with her best smile, hoping to wipe the scowl from Riko's face. "Someone said you were a musician."

"That's right." Riko twisted the little white wand to open the venetian blinds. The thin metal scraped as the strips revolved and diffused sunlight from the concrete courtyard crept across the room. Musical keyboards, computer keyboards and other unfamiliar electronic boxes were piled high on the monitor table and strung together with wires like a patient on life support. The walls were pale and the adjoining wall to Tamsin's flat was lined with neat shelves of books, games and records. Unlike the gloominess of Flat 1, the space was calm and light.

"Is it for a movie? A horror movie?"

"Nah." Riko took another drag from her cigarette and a trail of smoke drifted from her mouth. On second glance, the light-coloured ceiling and walls had a slight yellow stain. "My own stuff. I've done soundtracks before though."

"Anything I'd know?"

"No one saw them," Riko said.

"Your style of music is really unusual," Tamsin said, continuing unperturbed. "I don't think I've heard anything like it before."

Riko shrugged.

"There are so many creative people in the building . . . are you a musician full-time?"

"Ha! You think I'd live here if I was Taylor Swift? I run a few night classes in composition at Victoria Uni. With the odd shift club DJing on the side."

"Composition?"

Riko jerked her thumb at a framed certificate on the wall. A Doctorate in Fine Arts and Music in the name of Riko Royle. Tamsin hid her blinks of surprise. A PhD? Didn't this make Riko legitimate? So why did Bunty, who raved about Radcliffe as a creative haven, have it in for her? Tamsin inspected Riko once again, looking for the reason why, as if it might be written on her face.

"Look I'm—"

"I'd like to hear your song again," Tamsin interrupted. "If that's okay."

Riko raised an eyebrow. "Promise you won't call the cops?"

"Sorry about that, but the screams were so realistic."

"It was . . ." Riko said and then drifted away. She frowned and then her attention snapped back into the room. "I don't usually share my work this early in the process. It's a bit rough but you've already heard most of it, I guess. Grab a seat if you want. I'll stop before the screaming starts."

Tamsin lowered herself into the long brown couch and the soft cushions sucked her in like quicksand. Riko clicked the mouse and tapped a few keys, then waves of electronic whirrs and whooshes slithered out of a set of three-foot high speakers.

Enveloped by the couch and the swirling futuristic sounds, Tamsin closed her eyes. The white-noise sputters and bass-deep rumbles were entwined with a mournful harp. The piece grabbed Tamsin and squashed her chest like a thick tight belt. What was this? What was she hearing? Music was something you sang along to, tunes about heartbreak or sex or dancing. This was something else, an unfamiliar language. She gripped her thighs with clawed fingers as the song tossed her about in alien waters.

She didn't hear it at first. She was too busy struggling to understand the music. It was hidden amongst the surging unnatural sounds and sharp jabs of lamenting strings. Until it came through like an unexpected punch in the face.

'Death is coming.'

Tamsin lurched as the Voice slid between the sounds, the familiar warning hissing through the speakers.

'Death is coming,' it repeated. Today its tone was smug.

Her heart galloped as she whipped around and stared at the speakers. Where was the high pitch squeal? Where was the nausea? The Voice had never appeared unannounced before.

"What the fuck?" Riko said and started tapping at a keyboard.

Tamsin gasped and reeled back into the couch. Another person heard the Voice? Her Voice. Why was it talking to Riko? And how did it get into her song?

She clenched her hands into fists.

"Where did you get that from?" she said with a snarl.

"I don't know what it is," Riko said, a quiver in her voice as she stabbed at the keys. "I didn't put it there."

"But you must have—"

"I have no fucking idea!" Riko stopped the music dead and replayed the track from the beginning. She left the computer desk and rushed over to press her ear close to the speaker.

Tamsin's heart raced as she waited for the Voice to return. As the song thumped and whooshed, and the seconds ticked by and there was no Voice, she began to tell herself she'd made it up. It hadn't been there at all. Then it started.

'Death is coming.'

She pinched her eyes closed, a vein pulsed in her temple. It was true, somehow her Voice had wormed its way into Riko's music.

57

A scream blasted out and Riko hurried from the speaker back to the keyboard. She stopped and replayed the song from the beginning. A burning sensation tore across Tamsin's chest as she glared at the back of Riko's head. Why had the Voice chosen Riko?

The walls were closing in. Tamsin stood up and blurted, "I should be going."

"Yeah. Bye," Riko said without looking up from the screen. Tamsin loitered for a moment, expecting something more from Riko. An apology perhaps, or an explanation? But she got nothing and let herself out, leaving Riko muttering and slipping on a pair of headphones.

Tamsin's hands were shaking when she closed her own front door. She put away her groceries, still in a daze, and when she was finished, despite the fact it was only five o'clock, she went straight to bed and pulled the sheets up over her head.

"Why her?" she cried.

And no one answered.

Chapter Five

Day Seven

The next day Tamsin stayed in bed. The endless heat had seeped into Radcliffe's brick walls, and now her flat was as hot as a kiln. After hours of tossing, head swarming with questions and stomach churning with dread, Tamsin dragged herself up out of the damp sheets. It was getting dark, she'd wasted the whole day.

Carrying her empty laundry basket, she passed Riko's door, and hot jealous needles jabbed into her chest. Why had the Voice chosen Riko?

In the courtyard, the dusk sky was violet, and her sheets and towels on the Hills Hoist were as crispy as toast. As she unpegged the washing, a slight breeze tickled over her exposed skin. The wind must have changed, the shifting refreshing air cooler than it had been for days. She tilted back her head and stretched her arms out wide.

Over on the picnic table, a tea-light candle flickered in a glass jar. The door into the building opened, and Cecily and Bunty strolled out.

"We meet again," Cecily said, a wicker basket hanging in the crook of her elbow. "Good timing. Wine o'clock."

"I'm not really . . ." Tamsin tugged at her oversized stained t-shirt and shapeless skirt. Clothes she'd thrown on to collect her washing and not an outfit she'd choose to wear for company. Bunty, in her crease-free floral dress, must be horrified. It was lucky, Tamsin had put on a bra.

"Join us to celebrate this small respite from the heat, Patricia," Bunty said.

"It's Tamsin, Grandma," Cecily said and rolled her eyes.

"Of course," Bunty said. "Come on Tamsin, I'll be insulted if you don't join us."

"And you don't want to be on the wrong side of Grandma." Cecily grinned and glanced over at the ground floor windows across the courtyard. Riko's windows.

Tamsin winced at the reminder of Riko, resentment welling up inside her again. A glass of wine could help her forget, even for a few moments. "If you're sure . . ."

Cecily twisted open the cap on the bottle of rosé, and Tamsin folded up her washing. She moved carefully and self-consciously, not used to folding her sheets with an audience, and then took a seat between them at the battered picnic table. As she took the glass of salmon-pink wine from Cecily's hand, her belly knotted. Three glasses in the basket? How did they know she would be here?

"Cheers!" Cecily said as their glasses clinked in the night air. "To new friends."

The rosé was ice-cold and a hint of hibiscus sparkled on Tamsin's tongue.

"Tamsin, my dear. How many days have you been here now?" Bunty said. Her wrinkled fingers and red nails toying with the stem of the glass. "How are you liking Radcliffe so far?"

"Aside from the dead rat?" Cecily added. Her grandmother shot her a dirty look and Cecily winked at Tamsin.

"To be honest, it was a bit hot inside today," Tamsin said then winced, remembering Bunty's special relationship with Radcliffe. Would her complaints sound like she was slagging off a friend?

"Wait til winter," Cecily said then pulled a face. "If you're here that long."

"Tomorrow is going to be over forty again," Bunty said. "And they say it'll be another three or four days at least until a proper cool change."

"Ugh. I think I'll have melted by then," Tamsin said and took another sip of wine.

"You should get a fan," Bunty said and Tamsin mumbled in agreement. Or move back to her house in the suburbs where she had air-conditioning at the press of a remote.

"Have you met everyone in the building now?" Bunty asked.

"All except Gail. I'm beginning to wonder whether she exists at all." Tamsin attempted a casual laugh. "Or maybe there's a ghost walking across my ceiling day and night." She waited for the others to laugh along with her.

Instead, Bunty nodded. "You wouldn't be the first to feel a presence here." Her voice was grave. "Poor old Radcliffe has seen a good many tragedies over her lifetime."

"Here we go," Cecily said with a smirk.

Tamsin leaned forward on her elbows. "Like what?"

"Have you felt anything strange? Any cold spots?"

"I wish." Tamsin smiled but her feeble joke was met with stony silence. In the darkened courtyard, the pale-yellow candlelight fluttered and licked over their faces.

"Perhaps over in the corner near the front door?" Bunty raised an eyebrow.

Tamsin tightened her lips. The spot where the word was carved into the wall. She shook her head. Until she inspected the wall again in brighter light, she would stay quiet.

"Of course, any house as old as Radcliffe . . . before normal people could afford medicines and hospitals . . . has death within its walls," Bunty said in a dramatic whisper. "But she's seen more than her fair share."

"Even in my flat?" Tamsin frowned.

"There was a particularly nasty suicide right in that spot. I think it was in the nineteen eighties. A man blew his head off with a gun. He wasn't even a resident."

Grey-green walls splattered with blood and brains flashed into Tamsin's mind, a chubby middle-aged man slumped in the corner. She reeled. But this man's death was blunt, and—no matter how tragic—irrelevant. He was not the reason why the Voice had beckoned her here.

Bunty continued. "Then there were the heroin years. Horrible. One poor girl was there for two weeks before anyone noticed she was dead. It was a terrible time, the late nineties. I was scared to leave my flat for all the druggies coming in and out of the front door."

"You haven't told me that story before?" Cecily wrinkled her nose. "How horrible."

An overdose wasn't right either, those deaths would hang over her head like a low sad cloud. There was something chaotic and feverish about the death that brought her here.

"So you haven't felt anything, Tamsin? Nobody watching you? Pity. I guess some people are more sensitive to these things than others."

Tamsin clenched her jaw. In Bunty's eyes, she was a boring straight-laced tax accountant. If only Bunty knew the truth of why she was here. Explanations would have to wait. Right now, Tamsin wasn't even sure if she still had the gift or if she wasn't just another weird woman in a weird building.

"Not only in yours but there was also the poor woman who killed her baby in Flat number three. Well before my time. Back when doctors blamed everything on hysterical women."

Cecily rolled her eyes. "Dinosaurs."

"They still do it today!" Tamsin exclaimed. Then she smoothed back her hair and cleared her throat. "What happened to her? The woman?"

"I'm not entirely sure. Prison, perhaps? As I said, it was before my time. I lived there for a short period." Bunty shuddered. "I never liked it. And it wasn't just me."

"You haven't always lived in number five?"

"Oh no, it took me fifteen years to work my way up to the top floor. I started off in your Flat, then into number three and finally the second floor. I had terrible nightmares the whole time I lived there, and I would feel these icy drafts, even during a heatwave like now. There was one particular resident, although to be frank she was one of those nervy types. Terribly chewed fingernails. Anyway she swore she'd regularly hear a woman crying in the bathroom."

Despite the balmy evening, a shiver ran down Tamsin's spine. Perhaps the footsteps weren't Gail's at all.

64

"Poor woman. The one who killed her baby, not the nervous Nellie. All alone for weeks and months with a screaming baby who wouldn't settle. No one to help or talk to."

"How did she do it?" Cecily asked and Tamsin was glad. This was the question she was too gutless to ask.

"She drowned her little boy in the bath. Then again, it could all be complete lies. Some people have very active imaginations." Bunty waved her hand and her empty glass. "Top-up, darling?"

Tamsin swallowed. Would she be able to sleep tonight with all these stories tossing around her head?

"After all these years, I'm used to this place," Bunty continued as Cecily refilled her glass. "All the strange bumps and creaks in the night, they're all part of Radcliffe's character. Don't you think it's odd that people are scared of the dead? Scared of ghosts?"

Tamsin shrugged.

"I think it's exciting." Bunty's eyes gleamed. She sat forward cradling her wine glass. "Shouldn't we feel blessed if we experience something? It means the dead are trying to communicate with us! And death is not the end!"

Tamsin tittered, and not ready to share her own experience with messages from the beyond, she changed the subject. "Late the other night I heard Gail go out the front door. It seems she does leave the house occasionally."

"Are you sure it's her?" Cecily winked. "It could be a ghost."

"I made a mistake once. That's how I met Riko," Tamsin said.

She waited for a reaction from Bunty but she was staring down at her fingers as she rolled her wine glass stem.

Tamsin continued. "Gail must like to walk at night when the streets are quiet."

"And search for dead rats?"

"Cecie!" Bunty said and then tutted. "It sounds very reckless to me. A lone woman walking at night."

"You haven't heard her before?" Tamsin said.

"Grandma sleeps like a log." Cecily grinned.

A strange expression passed over Bunty's face, the look of a forlorn girl visible under her aged skin. She gazed around the brick walls and the concrete courtyard, her blue eyes vacant and puzzled.

Cecily raised the chilled bottle. "Another?"

Tamsin covered her glass with her hand. "One is plenty."

"How refreshing," Bunty said, snapping back to the conversation. "There have been more than enough alcoholics and drug addicts in that flat over the years. Perhaps you're here to cleanse Flat number one."

"And here I was thinking I'd disappointed you with my lack of creativity."

"Nonsense. As long as you pay your rent and you're a considerate resident, you could be a lawyer for all I care!"

They all laughed and Cecily replenished her Grandma's glass.

A light flickered on in an upstairs window.

"Oh, Defne is home," Bunty said.

"Just ignoring us," Cecily added.

"She must be in one of her moods. If there's one thing Radcliffe has taught me, we must respect each other's privacy."

If only that were true. Despite the open air, Tamsin was all of a sudden gripped by claustrophobia. Radcliffe was more crowded than she ever expected.

Chapter Six

Day Eight

Rubbing her scratchy eyes, Tamsin stared at the wall and wondered what Riko was doing on the other side. Riko, the one who'd heard her Voice, the only other person who had ever heard it.

"Why her?" she said aloud again.

Nothing she'd learned about her Gift from her research and forum friends explained how the Voice appeared in the song. Bewildered, Tamsin turned to her mentor, a person she knew only as the Angel Listener and poured the whole Radcliffe story out into a lengthy email.

Now her phone sat on the kitchen bench beside her, face-up, and every few moments her gaze darted to the black screen, hoping for a reply.

She stirred sugar into her mug and took a sip. She hadn't slept well, her mind a merry-go-round all night. The coffee scalded her mouth but she didn't care. Hot beverages in this weather made no sense, but her craving for caffeine shoved logic aside every time.

The kitchen backdoor had one small square window fitted with rippled safety glass, threaded with wire, and led out into the narrow passageway alongside the house. Weak yellow light sauntered through the clouded square. Was the door designed to keep others out or keep the tenants in?

And in between her thoughts of the Voice and Riko, Bunty's grim stories about the house trickled through. Overdoses, suicide, murder. How many people had died within these walls? She needed to know more.

Someone knocked at the flat front door and Tamsin groaned. With her mussed-up hair, skimpy nightie and saggy boobs, company was the last thing she wanted. Could she be like Gail and ignore the door? She smirked to herself and didn't move, taking another mouthful of coffee instead.

They knocked again. She presumed it would be their last and opened the fridge. She wasn't hungry but picked up a pot of mango yoghurt. The blast of cool air was like manna from heaven and she closed her eyes as it wafted over her bare skin.

Scratching sounds from elsewhere in the flat made Tamsin stop and turn her head. It was coming from the lounge room. She closed the fridge and tip-toed towards the noise.

Someone was opening her door. The handle turned and Tamsin froze. A man appeared in the open doorway, tall in a blue coverall with a smooth bald head and eyes like sinkholes.

"Who are you?" she stuttered.

"She told me to come," he said in a voice so deep, it rumbled in the bottom of her belly.

69

"Who?" she wheezed. "Death?"

He stepped inside, his boot clumped across the floorboards, a sports bag in his hand. "Upstairs," he said in his thunder-like rumble.

"Bunty?" she said with an exhale.

"The old one." With his creased face and hair sprouting from his nostrils, he wasn't exactly young himself. He put down his bag.

"You're the handyman?"

He nodded with his black cesspool eyes.

Tamsin pressed her lips together. "Someone could have warned me." Later, she would complain to Bunty.

"I thought no one was home."

"Well, I'm here." Tamsin folded her arms. This had the unintended effect of squeezing her breasts together, and once she realised she dropped her arms.

He shrugged. "She said you've got mice?"

"In here," she grumbled. He followed her into the kitchen with a waft of mint, an unsuccessful attempt to mask the underlying reek of tobacco and sweat. "I found a rat in the sink. It was huge."

He wrenched open the cupboard under the sink and got down on hands and creaking knees. Tamsin returned to her coffee and stood back to watch the bald old man root around inside. He muttered to himself as he leaned in deeper, and then emerged to open all the lower cupboards one by one.

"Have you worked here long?" she asked.

"Donkey's years." He groaned up to his feet and looked behind the fridge, then along all the skirting boards. She pressed her lips together. Given the general state of Radcliffe, she didn't have high hopes for his skills.

"As long as Bunty?"

"Longer."

Tamsin raised her eyebrows. "You would've seen a lot of change then?"

He shrugged. "I can't see any holes in the wall. You want a trap?"

"If you have one," she said. "I know it's hot outside but would you like a coffee?"

His head lifted. He stared at her with his black soulless eyes and a broad handsome smile bloomed over his face. "That would be great."

Tamsin scooped coffee into the moka pot and set it on the hot plate.

"If the trap doesn't work, I know a man who can help," he said as he unzipped his sports bag and set a trap under the sink. "Weird bloke. Knows everything about rats. Sells them to pet shops."

A few minutes later, he straightened up and she handed him a cup of steaming coffee. They stood side-by-side leaning up against the cabinets, Tamsin and the veteran maintenance man nursing mugs in their hands. She chewed on her lip. Her chance was short, she had as much time as there was coffee in his mug.

"I hear that Radcliffe has had a colourful past," she began.

"Lots of people have lived here over the years."

Tamsin licked her lips and chose her words with care. "And a few . . . spooky things?"

"I thought I saw something once, a few years back, down there under the stairs. I was drinking a bit in those days. Not now though."

"The ghosts are gone?"

"Nah, the booze."

Tamsin tried again. "You and Bunty are old friends, then?"

"I remember when she first came here. Pretty. Now she's old like me. But she was always up herself. Full of fancy stories. Most of it made up, I reckon."

Tamsin hid a smirk with a sip.

"In all these years, she's never made me a coffee."

She winced.

"I'm not bothered," he continued. "There's something weird about her. Always was."

"What do you mean?"

72

"She scares me."

Tamsin studied the old man as he stared into his mug. The men in her life would never admit fear to a stranger.

"There's something behind her eyes." He took a long noisy slurp.

"What do you—?"

He placed the empty mug down on the counter with a clunk. "I better be off."

"Oh. I was hoping you could look at the window in my bedroom. I can't get it open."

"I'll come back another time. Thanks for the coffee." He was already halfway out the kitchen door.

"Next time, make sure you knock three times. So I know it's you."

He waved without turning back and the front door closed soon after.

Tamsin's shoulders slumped. Could she believe anything anyone said in this house? And she forgot to ask if he had a step ladder she could borrow.

#

Alone again, Tamsin sat down on the lounge room floor with a notebook and her mementoes. All these stories about Radcliffe had distracted her from the real reason she was here, she needed to focus. She set all five items out on the ground in a circle and

73

stared at them one by one. A single gold dangle earring of Bunty's, a white ankle sock belonging to Cecily, a spoon from Defne's kitchen, one of Riko's cigarette butts, and an envelope addressed to Gail. All five women spread out around her. Five lives and five potential deaths. She focused on a blank page in her notebook until the blue lines turned into squiggles, and then at her collection one by one. She waited, hoping for a bolt of insight, or the Voice to appear and point out the woman she should be helping. But there was nothing, only a thirty-eight year old woman sprawled on the floor of a ramshackle house, as lost and confused as ever.

#

Sick of sitting in the flat feeling useless, Tamsin ventured out into the heat to learn more about the strange building she currently called home. While she suspected the handyman was right and Bunty's stories were more embellished than Christmas, there was no doubt a house as old as Radcliffe would be familiar with death. And maybe the past held a clue.

Tamsin trudged through the streets, her bare white skin like pork belly in the oven under the blistering sun. She darted from shadow to shadow, under trees and awnings, desperate for any brief respite from the scalding rays.

After the sweltering ten minute walk, she stepped into the air-conditioned comfort of the State Archives Centre. A dapper

74

young man behind the reception desk offered to help with a warm smile.

"I'm looking for information about a building," she said, fanning her moist face with her hand, and within minutes, she was huddled over a computer, trawling the records for references to Radcliffe. First she flicked through maps and narrowed down the dates when Radcliffe was built, sometime between 1879 and 1882, when North Melbourne was synonymous with slums. In the council records, she found Peregrine Inchcombe, who must have been a relation of Gideon Inchcombe, the owner Bunty mentioned.

She moved onto old digitised newspapers and then the stories began to stack up.

Guilty - Murder in the Dosshouse (1931) The Argus.

Raid on notorious brothel (1952) The Sun Pictorial.

Heroin epidemic - woman not found for a week (1997) The Herald Sun.

There was enough evidence of death and scandal here to validate many of Bunty's tales, but none of the names were familiar and there was nothing about an infanticide or suicides. Then again Tamsin had heard that newspapers never printed those types of stories, for fear of copycats. Or maybe that was just another urban myth.

The final icing on the cake came from the less salubrious broadsheet of the 1970s - The Truth - *A Ghost got me pregnant*.

Tamsin pushed back in her chair and chewed her pen. All this was interesting, but it was leading her nowhere. She turned her attention to her neighbours, her first search was for Bunty. A professional dancer would surely show up somewhere in print, but a search for 'Bunty Hetherington' produced nothing. Maybe she was not as successful as she claimed, a low-ranking chorus girl wouldn't warrant a mention.

The next enigma was Gail. This time, Tamsin turned to the free WIFI and searched on her phone for LG McGovern. She flicked through reviews and bookshop websites until she came across her author site, a clean and welcoming blog listing all her books, but with a very vague bio. Tamsin's finger hovered over the 'Contact Me' link but she scrolled away before she made a fool of herself. Over on her author Facebook page, Gail chatted with her avid fans, who were desperate to get their hands on her next release. Her books had to be the way in with Gail, the final resident and last piece of the puzzle at Radcliffe.

#

Too hot to sleep, Tamsin lay on her couch with a cold flannel on her forehead and Gail's book in her hand. Druid's Kiss, the story of the forbidden love between the inquisitive daughter of the local Lord and a flame-haired novice druid, was so engrossing that Tamsin almost missed the thump of footsteps down the stairs.

Gail? She hadn't heard the door close above her head. Maybe it was Defne or Cecily. Although while a uni student in her prime partying years, she'd never heard Cecily leave the house at night. And while verging on middle age, Defne was the same. There appeared to be two shifts in Radcliffe, the day walkers and the night walkers, and this had to be Gail heading out on one of her midnight excursions.

No one in Radcliffe knew the truth about Gail, where she went or what she did. Like Riko said it was a game, and the other residents spun their own embellished tales, each wilder than the last, to fill in the gaps. She was beginning to see that Gail was not the only mystery in the house, the walls of Radcliffe were painted with secrets and obfuscation. There was a lot more going on under the surface than anyone would admit. Herself included.

She dropped Druid's Kiss onto the floor and sat up. Over half-way through the book, now she had a conversation starter with Gail. She couldn't launch straight into asking where she went, and what the police had wanted. And whether death was coming for her.

Tamsin scurried up off the couch but when she opened her door, the building's front door was already swinging shut. She turned back, shoved sneakers onto her bare feet and set off after Gail.

Outside, the night air was warm and sticky. Up ahead, an apple-shaped woman with cropped hair disappeared around the corner into Lachlan Street. Tamsin sped up, keeping one eye out for Gail—or at least the woman she presumed was Gail—and another eye out for any strange men lurking in the shadows.

Despite her hunger to catch Gail, Tamsin had forgotten to check the author photograph on the inside cover of Druid's Kiss before she left. If this woman was Gail, she was not at all what Tamsin expected. In a sleeveless linen shirt and lavender mid-calf trousers, Gail looked like a suburban woman out for a bit of shopping, rather than the glamorous spy or gangster's wife. And yet, she had poise, striding down the badly lit street as if it were the middle of the day. Tamsin, in contrast, held her handbag in a death grip and flinched at the tiniest of sounds.

Gail then turned into a narrow laneway, her sandals clattering across the bluestone cobbles. Between terrace houses, the alley was the type of darkened secluded place Tamsin would never venture on her own at night. With a deep breath in, she followed.

Passing wheelie bins, piles of dog turds and high fences with razor wire, she crept behind Gail until she slipped on the uneven stones. She rolled her ankle, losing her balance, and banged her shoulder into a roller door tagged with graffiti. The clang roused a dog who snarled and clawed on the other side of the metal door. She jumped back, and then froze, waiting for Gail to turn around and spot her. Tamsin scrambled for excuses but Gail didn't look back and, after a few seconds, Tamsin exhaled and continued her pursuit.

The lane ended, opening up onto the bright white street lights of the Errol Street shopping strip. Staying in the shadows, Tamsin paused at the end of the alley and watched Gail cross the road under the overhanging tram wires. Gail continued along the other side of the street, passing hipster cafes, boutique bottle shops and beauty salons closed up for the night, until she ducked inside the all-night convenience store. Tamsin followed her, jogging across the road and stopping outside the shop with its flashing neon sign. She glimpsed her reflection in the window. Her hair was slathered like limp lettuce against her face, her loose dress ringed with underarm sweat. This was not how she pictured her first meeting with Gail.

The automatic doors opened and Tamsin blinked into the eye-aching brightness. On the left, a drunk couple were arguing by the slushy machine, while Gail strode down the middle aisle, scanning the shelves purposefully.

As the sweat cooled on her skin, Tamsin loitered by the cold drinks fridge and practiced her opening line.

"Hi. I think we're neighbours."

"You look familiar, do you live at Radcliffe?"

"Are you LG McGovern?"

Every idea sounded creepier and more awkward than the last. Rather than making a fool of herself, Tamsin hunched her shoulders and made a bee-line for the ice-cream freezer. She grabbed a tropical icy-pole, a childhood favourite, paid the androgynous olive-skinned person behind the clear plastic shield and headed back outside into the heat.

As she tore open the wrapper, she decided to hang back out of sight and follow Gail all the way home. As usual, Tamsin was sure she was inconspicuous, just another insomniac on a stinking hot Melbourne night, treating herself to an ice cream. Pineapple juice rolled down her fingers as the icy-pole started to melt.

"Any spare change?" a woman with a sun-ravaged face and a broken front tooth asked. Tamsin slurped the sweet stickiness off her fingers and fished a dollar coin out of her handbag. Inside, Gail was at the counter with a six-pack of eggs and a strawberry-flavoured milkshake. Breakfast? Surely the mysterious Gail would be up to something more interesting.

Then the doors whooshed open and Gail marched out, her purchases swinging from a reusable shopping bag on her wrist. Her eyes lifted and met Tamsin's for a split second. Tamsin flinched and glanced away, but not before she caught a shimmer in Gail's brown eyes. There was only one way to describe what she'd seen—mischief, pure and simple. If it was possible, Tamsin was now even more curious about her neighbour.

Gail strode off again, but rather than taking the same route back, she set off in the opposite direction. Tamsin sucked the remaining slush off the wooden icy-pole stick and frowned. Eggs. Breakfast for two? Was Gail off to see her lover? She expected it was nothing less than a steamy and torrid affair with a much younger man or woman. Tamsin tossed the stick in the bin and went after her.

Her neighbour wove through the deserted side streets with a determined stride, not looking over her shoulder once. After another ten minutes of walking, Tamsin was lost and wondered if Gail was tricking her, leading her in circles, but soon Gail stopped outside a two-storey house in a narrow street.

The plain beige new-build townhouse was wedged between two grand Victorian terraces. Upstairs, the blinds were wide open and light beamed out across the street, a bright rectangle in the darkness while the rest of the street slept. Gail crossed to the opposite footpath and stared at the lit-up window while Tamsin stayed back, crouching behind a parked Volvo.

Minutes passed and Gail stood there, looking up. Not moving. Not calling anyone or ringing the doorbell, just watching, patiently, attentively.

A bald man's silhouette appeared. He pushed open the window. "Get out of here, Gail," he yelled.

She didn't blink and stood like a sentry, with arms folded, while a dog barked in the distance.

"I'm sick of this," he continued. "For God's sake. Leave us alone."

"Never!" she bellowed. Her voice clear and deep.

"Not you again!" A fat woman dressed only in her bra and knickers was standing at a Juliet balcony above Gail's head, mobile phone clutched in her hand. "Fuck off, will ya?"

Ignoring them both, Gail reached inside her shopping bag and flung an egg at the bald man's window. Yellow and white goo splattered against the glass. Fragments of shell dropped onto the footpath and Gail cackled. She plucked out a second egg, this time aiming for the front door of the townhouse.

"That's it! I'm calling the cops!" he cried and slammed the window shut.

Gail sprinted towards his front door and pulled the whole carton of eggs out of her bag. She scrunched the remaining eggs between her fingers and shoved the slimy mixture through the letterbox slot. Next she shook the plastic bottle of flavoured milk and poured pink slime all over the blue hatchback parked out the front.

Behind the Volvo, Tamsin clapped her hand over her mouth.

The town house door opened and a small woman in a scarlet kimono rushed out onto the street. "Gail. Please."

"Don't!" yelled the man from inside. "Don't even try."

"Please. This has gone on long enough," the petite woman said, wringing her hands.

"Not til you apologise," Gail snapped.

"How many times do we have to tell you? We didn't do anything."

"Liars!" Gail screeched. Her voice bounced off the windows and walls of the built-up street. "Liars!" She threw the empty carton and plastic bottle down onto the footpath and stomped away.

"Good riddance," yelled the half-naked neighbour. "Don't worry, darl. I recorded her this time."

"Thank you," the woman in the kimono sniffed, and with slumped shoulders, retreated inside.

Soon, the street was dead quiet again. Tamsin stayed put in her hiding place, giving Gail a head start back home. While she waited, she pulled out her mobile and noted down the address of the house now coated in raw egg. What had these people done to Gail?

#

Thirty minutes later, she was back at Radcliffe, sweating. The lights upstairs in Flat 3 were on. She slid her key into the lock and stepped inside without turning on the hallway light. A delicious cold shower was only seconds away.

She closed the front door softly behind her. Not only out of courtesy for those sleeping in the house, but also to hide the fact from Gail. It was ridiculous but somehow Tamsin felt Gail would know. And if she'd learned one thing tonight, it was that making Gail mad was a bad idea.

"I tried . . ." A voice moaned in the shadows. ". . . but I couldn't."

Tamsin jumped. Her keys slipped out of her hand and hit the linoleum with a dull clunk.

"Who's there?"

Her heart galloped as she squinted into the dark and all the infamous stories about Radcliffe came surging back.

"It won't let me leave," the voice pleaded.

"Bunty?" Tamsin frowned. "Is that you?"

She flicked on the light switch. Bunty was sitting on a step halfway up the stairs, in her floral nightie with her long white hair loose and flowing down to her waist.

"Are you alright?" Tamsin said.

"She takes hold of you and won't let go." Her blue eyes were blank and staring.

"Who?"

"You know who." She glanced up with a scoff. "I should have warned you. I should have never let you move in here. Any of you. You'll all end up like me. They should board the place up and let it rot. Or better yet, bulldoze it!" She gripped the bannister with a thickly-veined hand.

"I thought you and the house were old friends." Tamsin inched towards the staircase, keeping her voice as calm as she could. "Where's Cecily?"

"Who?"

"Your granddaughter? Should we get you back to bed?" Tamsin mounted the stairs. "It's very late."

The old woman grumbled and Tamsin took her hand and helped her up to her feet. Bunty's hands were ice-cold, unnaturally so, and even inside the hot airless house, Tamsin shuddered.

"Where's your stick?"

Bunty didn't reply. She hoisted herself up the stairs, one step at a time. Tamsin rushed to her side and clutched her elbow.

After a few minutes of struggling, they arrived at the first landing and Tamsin's brow was damp all over again. She led Bunty around to the second flight of stairs, but Bunty pulled away and hobbled for the door to Flat 3.

"No. This way," Tamsin said, recalling Bunty's terrible story about the infanticide. "You don't live there anymore."

"This is where I live. Where I will live forever."

"Come on, Bunty, up this way. You're on the top floor now."

"Grandma!" Cecily appeared at the top of the landing in tiny shorts and a tank-top. She hurried down the steps to grab her grandmother's arm. "You scared the life out of me. What are you doing wandering about?"

Bunty mumbled and hung her head like a scolded child.

"Do you need any help?" Tamsin said, feeling useless all of a sudden, as Cecily guided Bunty upstairs.

"I can look after her from here," Cecily said. "But thank you. Imagine if she'd made it out the front door." She grimaced, then turned back to her grandmother. "Let's get you back to bed. Naughty Bunty."

The two women, one with long white hair, the other with brown curls headed up the remaining stairs.

Tamsin's heart ached. Up until this moment, Bunty had been so vivacious. Like death, ageing was coming for them all.

Chapter Seven

Day Nine

The next day, Tamsin slept until late morning. Once or twice she'd woken in the night with her chest clenched, sensing a pair of red hot eyes fixed on her as she slept. But there was no one there. She blamed a combination of the heat and Bunty's strange ramblings last night on the stairs. Earlier in the week, Cecily had mentioned Bunty's poor health, but Tamsin had assumed it was physical. She sighed. How terrible it must be to watch someone you love deteriorate. She hid her fading health well but at night, her ghosts must return.

Now wide awake, Tamsin pulled her notebook out from the fridge and climbed back into bed to update her notes on Gail. Who were the couple in the house? The bald man appeared around the same age as Gail while the woman was definitely younger. There was one obvious well-trodden explanation for why a woman would trash a man's house in the middle of the night. Betrayal. The dark-haired woman in the kimono must be Gail's replacement. Tamsin chewed on her pen. She needed to get closer to Gail, but how?

Lost for ideas, she turned to Bunty's page, hesitating before she wrote anything down. Her eyes flickered to the adjacent page.

Riko. Her jaw tightened. Every time she recalled the words in Riko's music, her heart crumpled. Why was the Voice there? What did it mean? Had she let the Voice down? Her throat thickened. She hadn't made any headway since arriving at Radcliffe. Had it forsaken her and found a new conduit? Was the Voice whispering to Riko right now, telling her everything? Tamsin clenched her fists, and for a moment, understood Gail.

She reached for her phone to check for a reply from the Angel Listener, but was interrupted by a knock at the door.

"Are you busy?" Defne was glowing. Her glossy black hair was slicked back, and as usual, her generous body enveloped in metres of flowing black fabric.

With a pained smile, Tamsin rubbed the back of her neck. This was the first time they'd met since the rat appeared in her sink. Defne's face was bright with excitement, and no matter how hard Tamsin looked, she couldn't see even a skerrick of malice. If she wasn't responsible for the rat, then who was?

"I was just reading Gail's book," Tamsin lied and pointed to Druid's Kiss lying on the floor where she'd left it last night. "What do you have in mind?"

"We're going out." Her eyes danced and she grabbed for Tamsin's hand with a clammy palm. "I've got something to show you."

"Now I'm curious," Tamsin replied and a genuine grin broke out on her face. She gestured at her shapeless blue striped dress and grimaced. "Do I need to dress up?"

"You're perfect as you are. Although you might need shoes."

Tamsin excused herself to the shabby bathroom. Butterflies scurried in her tummy as she checked her reflection in the tarnished mirror. She combed her hair and sprayed on a little perfume, she'd given up on make-up years earlier. Whatever this occasion was, it would be important enough to smell nice for.

They shut the front door and stepped out into the treacle-like heat. Tamsin groaned as her forehead slickened with sweat.

Defne bounced her keys in her hand and loitered by a white Hyundai parked outside Radcliffe. Tamsin's heart skipped at the possibility of air conditioning.

"No," Defne said. "Let's walk."

Tamsin kept her disappointment to herself.

As they walked through the scorching afternoon heat, Defne babbled on without revealing where they were going, twiddling the three rings on her left hand. "I'm so glad to have someone to share this with."

Didn't Defne have other friends? People she'd known longer than five days? Although the same thing could be said about Tamsin. These days, her entire social circle lived online. When she first mentioned her online community to Abby, and how pleased she was to find other auditory psychics who understood what she was going through, her sister looked at her with pity. Online friends weren't real friends, Abby said. She couldn't be more wrong. Tamsin's online community was her rock and one day she'd fly to Birmingham, Missoula and Hyderabad to meet her friends face to face. Anyway, she couldn't expect Abby to understand. Her sister had probably never felt a second of loneliness in her entire life.

#

A few minutes later, Tamsin and Defne arrived on Errol Street. The pedestrians moved at half speed through the heat, plodding through the thick air. The tram tracks were ribbons of molten silver in the sun and the end of the street shimmered like an interdimensional portal. They continued down the street until Defne stopped and pushed open a door between a pharmacist and a bottle shop.

"A tattoo shop?" Tamsin said, then scanned Defne for signs of ink. Perhaps this was a trip for a new tattoo and Tamsin was there to hold her hand, or help her choose a design. Either way, Tamsin felt unqualified for the job.

"Come in." Defne's eyes glistened as they stepped inside a long narrow hallway. "Here we are! Here I am!"

The walls were lined with mounted black and white photographs, the size of wide screen televisions.

"You?" Tamsin gasped.

Defne thrust her chin in the air. "You're looking at my first ever solo exhibition."

Tamsin copied Defne's smile until her gaze stopped on the nearest picture. A blow-up of a woman's hand, fingernails broken and jagged. The nail on her middle finger was split and bloodied, ripped right through the centre and all the way to the cuticle. And on the ring finger, a metal nail file was shoved between the skin and the nail. Tamsin winced and curled her fingers into a ball. The small white card underneath read *Manicure*.

She wandered down the hallway, taking in each piece, one by one. *Cankle* was a pyre of hoofs, or perhaps pigs trotters, scorched and blackened with ashes. The next one, *Me Time* featured rotting fish heads with dead milky eyes floating in a bubble bath. The fourth photo was a close-up of an open mouth, ringed with lipstick and filled with matted hair and soap, like the gunk pulled from a shower drain. Tamsin's stomach curdled. All these disturbing images came from inside Defne's head? She took a deep breath, then turned back to Defne with a pasted-on smile.

"Oh my god . . . Tamsin . . . look." Defne skipped down the hallway to a photo with a red dot underneath. She screamed and clutched at her throat. "I've sold one! I've sold a photo in my own exhibition." She dissolved into gasping sobs.

"That's good, isn't it?" Tamsin sidled up to her and fished a tissue from her handbag. The sold photo was of a dead cow's head. A torn threadbare teddy bear had one foot inside the mouth, the long cow's tongue lolled from the other side. Tamsin swallowed.

"It's wonderful," Defne said with a choke. "For so many years I hid my creativity. I was desperate to become an artist but people like me weren't photographers. But look. Look at that red dot. I'm an artist now. A real artist." She covered her face with her hands. Her whole black-clad body heaved and Tamsin loitered by her side, holding out the tissue.

A door at the opposite end of the hallway opened.

"And here she is!" A man with a neat grey beard, black round spectacles and a crisp white shirt rolled up to the elbows said. "I don't have to ask whether you've seen it. Congratulations, my darling."

"Oh Terry." Defne dropped her hands. Trails of black mascara trickled down her cheeks and Tamsin handed her a tissue discreetly. "Thank you so much for letting me exhibit here."

"A pleasure, my dear. Truly. I'm not just saying that. Our customers love your work. And it's weeding out the ones we don't want. Turning away those who can't cope with true, pure, raw art like this. You're doing me a favour, believe me. I wouldn't want to touch anyone who can't appreciate genius like yours."

Tamsin surveyed Terry up and down. The skin on his forearms, face and neck were pristine and unblemished by tattoos. He owned a tattoo shop?

"You're too kind." Defne dabbed at her eyes and then introduced Tamsin.

"You have a very talented friend here," he said. "Now, Defne, my lovely, I would take you out for a celebratory drink but I've got a full book tonight and I need a steady hand. Let's catch up next week. By then of course, everything will be sold, and it will be your shout."

They roared with laughter and Tamsin joined in with a forced chuckle.

"This is definitely a cause for celebration." Defne clutched at Tamsin's arm.

"Absolutely," Tamsin replied. "Drinks on me."

Saying goodbye to Terry, they went out into the relentless heat once more and found a cosy wine-bar close by, as deliciously cold as a cave and lined with second-hand books. With a glass of Prosecco each, they found a table for two and toasted Defne's new success.

"I still can't believe it." Defne sighed as she leaned back in her chair. "I've had a few pieces in group exhibitions. I've sold one or two, but I thought they were flukes. This is real."

Tamsin gave an enthusiastic nod but wondered whether she'd ever be able to forget those creepy images. What type of person would buy them? And what would they do with them? Would they hang them on their lounge room walls next to the television and Christmas tree? She hid a shudder and switched topics to another question burning on her tongue.

"Tell me about Terry? He owns the tattoo shop, right? But I couldn't see any tattoos on him."

"I know. Isn't it weird?" Defne said. "I asked him about it once, and he just winked."

Tamsin laughed with an accidental snort.

"Makes you curious, doesn't it?" Defne arched a dark eyebrow. "Makes you want to find out for yourself. I think he's gay though. Anyway, at our age, men are more trouble than they're worth. You do like men, don't you?"

"Um . . . yes," Tamsin replied. "Well, some of them."

"I don't care if you don't. Anything goes these days." She gestured at the younger hipper crowd in the bar, all different hairstyles and genders and fashions, yet all looking at their phones. "Isn't it great? Of course, silly me. You're divorced."

Tamsin pressed her lips together and nodded, glad of the reminder about her fake ex-husband. "I'm not ready to get into anything yet. But today is not about me. This is your big day . . . so what's next for you? The National Gallery?"

"Please." Defne scoffed. "I am just over the moon that someone liked my work enough to buy it. I sit all alone in my flat every day, trying to get the images right. To capture exactly what I see in my head in the frame. Some days—most days—it's like trying to grab a handful of steam. I know what I want, the reaction I want from the image, but I can never quite grasp it. It drives me half-mad, you know."

Again Tamsin nodded but had no idea what Defne meant.

Defne let out a long exhale and reached across the table to pat Tamsin's hand. "Please don't take it personally if I'm a bit all over the shop sometimes. I know I can get a bit intense when I'm in the middle of a difficult piece."

"They're quite . . . dark . . . ." Tamsin hesitated. "I can see how you might get absorbed."

"Thank you! I've always liked weird things but I could never express myself the way I wanted to when I was married. Or even before, growing up with my family. So traditional." Defne rolled her big brown eyes. "I always envied the arty kids at school, the punks, the goths, free to try whatever they wanted. No father and mother breathing down their necks. Or a community of busy-

95

bodies telling on you if you even spoke to an Anglo boy in the street."

Tamsin nodded. "I was always a little scared of the alternative kids. I can be a bit of a wuss though. I can't even cope with horror movies."

"No, really? I love them. I have heaps of giallo blu-rays at home."

"Giallo?"

"Seventies Italian horror. They're the best. You must come round and watch them with me."

"No way."

"You can hide behind the couch if you want. I'll warn you when the scary bits are coming."

They laughed and Defne went to the bar for another round. Usually a second drink wasn't a good idea but this was a special occasion, and Tamsin held her tongue. She couldn't remember the last time she made a new friend. In real life, that is. Perhaps she was wrong about the rat. It must have been someone else. Or it crawled into her sink all by itself.

Defne returned with two fresh fizzing flutes. "If my father saw me now. A woman drinking in public. How shameful." She laughed and handed a glass to Tamsin. "Stuff him. Today is all about me."

"And the first of many successful solo exhibitions," Tamsin toasted and they clinked glasses. "You'll have to prepare yourself for all the attention from the media. Interviews on all those arty shows on the ABC." She leaned forward with her fist clenched like a microphone. Her voice turned mock serious. "Tell us Defne, what inspired your latest exhibition?"

With a giggle, Defne smoothed back her dark hair and straightened her posture. "Why thank you, Tamsin. I'm glad you asked. I've always been a fan of the macabre and the grotesque. In today's culture with our perfectly curated and filtered lives, we try to hide the mess and the blood. But leave a piece of fruit out on the bench too long and see what happens—watch decay take hold. Maybe I'm not like other people but I find the disgusting beautiful. You know what's at the core of all this? We're pretending that we'll live forever. We try to convince ourselves we're never going to be that blackening banana. We're too scared to face up to the fact that death is coming for all of us."

Death is coming. The phrase clanged in Tamsin's head like a klaxon. The carefree moment with a new friend had gone.

"Death is coming for us . . ." Defne continued. "No matter how many sit-ups we do. Buddhists observe the five remembrances, meditations on the reality of ageing, illness and dying . . ."

Death is coming. Tamsin drifted back to the line of unsettling photographs but she struggled to recall them in real detail. Defne tossed her head and kept talking while Tamsin studied her face. Could it be true? Like Riko, was the Voice visiting Defne as well?

Chapter Eight

Day Ten

The next morning, Cecily knocked on Tamsin's door. Her usual golden complexion was ashen, her green eyes dull and underscored with dark circles.

"Are you okay?" Tamsin asked. "Has something happened to Bunty?"

"I thought I should explain."

Tamsin's pulse raced. At last someone was coming to her with information. "Come in. Please."

Cecily's usual grace was gone, she plodded inside and slumped onto the couch. She dropped her slouchy handbag onto the ground, pinched the bridge of her nose and waved away the offer of a drink. "I'm worried about her . . . her sleep-walking. I can't get her to talk to a doctor about it."

Tamsin grimaced. "She seemed wide awake to me. Definitely confused, but not sleep walking."

Cecily exhaled and shook her head.

"Does she remember it happening?"

"It's hard to tell. She fobs me off when I ask. She's really stubborn sometimes."

"That's hard. What does your mum think?"

Cecily blinked. "My mother?"

"Have you talked to your mum about this?"

"No," Cecily scoffed then looked away.

"Sorry." Tamsin's cheeks flushed. "I assumed Bunty was your mum's mum. There might be family history. Or she's been ill before?"

"They don't talk. I don't talk to my mum either. I tracked Bunty down all on my own a few years ago. I'd never met her before then. Now, she's the only real family I've got."

"I'm sorry."

"Don't be. We don't get to choose our families. At least I've got Bunty. For now." Cecily paused with a sad smile. "Thanks for helping her."

"It was nothing."

"I hope she didn't wake you up."

"No," Tamsin said, then clamped her mouth shut before she said too much. She knew how weird the truth sounded. It was a shame because the story of Gail and the eggs was dancing on her tongue, desperate to be shared. Instead, she chose a safe half-truth. "I was still up."

"Good. Thank god, you're here. It's nice to have someone around who's reliable."

Tamsin went to protest but as she flicked through the faces of the others in the house, she realised Cecily was probably right.

"You know, I feel better already," Cecily continued. "A problem shared or whatever they say. I'm embarrassed to admit I don't have many friends. I moved here from the country to study and it also gave me a chance to find Grandma."

Tamsin blinked. A country girl? She seemed so sophisticated.

"You look tired," Tamsin said. "All these hot nights. It's so hard to sleep."

"The weird thing is I've been sleeping really deeply the last few nights. Too deep. I didn't hear her get up. Lucky, you were there. If she'd wandered outside . . ."

Tamsin nodded, her brow creased with imagined bad endings.

Cecily leaned in. "What did she say to you?"

"Nothing really . . . a few things about Radcliffe."

"Talking about the building like it's a person? That's classic Bunty. I've been reading up on it from a psychological perspective." Cecily's face brightened a bit. "Personification. People who feel sympathy for objects. Fascinating, but totally harmless."

"This time was different. Usually she talks about the building like a friend. She said the place should be knocked down."

Cecily's eyebrows rose. "I've never heard Grandma say anything like that before."

"She said I should have never moved here."

"Interesting. How do you feel about that?"

"Me? Worried, of course."

"You're regretting moving here?"

"Not worried for me. Worried for Bunty. It must be horrible to get confused like that."

"Are you happy here?"

"I guess." Tamsin forced out a chuckle. "I've never lived anywhere where I've known all my neighbours like this. Especially so soon."

"It is a bit unusual. Do you think you'll stay long?"

"I have no idea."

Everything depended on the Voice. Her absent friend.

Cecily nodded. "Who knows what tomorrow brings," she said and got up to her feet. "I should get going. I've got a lecture."

As she stood up, she knocked over her handbag. Everything inside tipped out onto the floor; pens, a wallet, a phone in a pink case. Tissue packs, a nail, a notebook. Earbuds in a case, three lip gloss tubes, silver coins. And a vial of pills.

Tamsin got down on her knees to help, and picked up the pill bottle, Cecily Mansour printed on the label.

Cecily grabbed the bottle but not before Tamsin glimpsed the word Benruka written in bold lettering. The name of the drug. "I better go. The lecturer is a real prick if anyone's late."

As soon as the front door closed and Cecily was gone, Tamsin pulled out her phone and searched Benruka. A sleeping pill she suspected. It turned out, she was wrong. Her mouth dropped open as she continued reading.

It was a medication for lymphoma.

Chapter Nine

Day Eleven

On Tuesday morning, Tamsin slipped a handwritten note under the doors of all the other flats.

> *Barbecue in the courtyard tomorrow night from 6.30pm to celebrate my first week in Radcliffe.*
> *Please bring a plate.*
> *Hope to see you there.*
>
> *Tamsin.*

Her plan was simple, a few drinks and dinner on neutral ground to loosen their tongues. So far, all her notebook jottings and character studies had led to nothing and now, with no other option, had resorted to a tried and true method, calling all the suspects into the drawing room to reveal the murderer.

Unlike with Poirot or Miss Marple, in this case the victim was the mystery and Tamsin still had no idea which of the five women was in danger. Hopefully, when they were all gathered together, the Voice would pipe up and point out the person she'd been sent to save. Then again, with the disturbing discovery of Cecily's pills, did she already know the answer? But Tamsin was powerless to stop a serious illness, it had to be someone, or something, else.

Wednesday arrived—yet another scorcher—and by the time Tamsin dried herself after her shower, she was damp with sweat all over again. None of her neighbours had responded or even mentioned her invitation, and all day she paced up and down, wearing a new path in the tattered kitchen linoleum. Would she be sitting out in the courtyard all alone later tonight? A friendless loser melting in the heat? It wouldn't be the first time.

Tamsin distracted herself with preparations. She threaded marinated lamb, onion and green capsicum onto wooden skewers and mixed up a batch of her signature tuna mousse dip. As it neared six o'clock, she ventured out to the balmy concrete courtyard and tried to ignore the metallic stink of rubbish curdling inside the wheelie bins around the corner. She spread a lacy tablecloth—a bargain from the local charity shop—onto the weather-beaten picnic table, and in the centre, placed a jar filled with sprigs of red bottlebrush. Her tummy fluttered as she smoothed down the cloth. How long had it been since she last entertained? Maybe the night when she told Abby about the Voice? A night she'd rather forget. She should call Abby before her sister reported her to the police. But another day wouldn't hurt, and an argument with her sister was the last thing she needed tonight.

A rusty barbecue lived in the corner of the courtyard, and yesterday–to her delight–she found the gas hose was still attached and picked up a full bottle from the Arden Street service station. Today, after a click and a twist of the knob, the tarnished barbecue sprung to life. As the blackened and crusted hot plate heated up, Tamsin scraped away the old fat with a scrunched-up newspaper and a spatula. She pressed her nose into her elbow as coils of acrid black smoke rose into the air.

"Wow," said a voice and the back door slammed. It was Riko with a small blue esky swinging from her elbow. "I always wondered whether that old heap worked."

Tamsin beamed. If Riko, the second most unlikely person to turn up was here, perhaps even Gail might make an appearance.

"So far so good," Tamsin said.

Riko took a seat on the rickety bench at the picnic table and flipped open a beer. The brown bottle hissed as the cap skipped across the table. She took a slurp. "First one to arrive, eh?"

"I was worried I'd be spending the night out here on my own." Tamsin laughed but the sound was needy and brittle.

"I needed a break." Riko necked her beer again. "The piece I'm working on is doing my fucking head in."

Tamsin's belly lurched. Had Riko been working on the song with the Voice? She itched to ask more but every question she had rehearsed made her sound like a possessive lover.

She joined Riko at the table and the back door swung open. Defne waddled out in another ankle-length shapeless black dress with a clunking green shopping bag in her hand.

Now there were two.

"Welcome," Tamsin chirped, then cringed. "Does that sound strange? It's your house more than mine."

"Course not." Defne slipped onto the bench opposite Riko and Tamsin tried to guess her mood. She was here, this was a positive sign, but her voice was clipped.

"Riko," Defne said with a flat formal tone, as she unpacked plastic containers from her bag with all the enthusiasm of a factory worker. "I haven't seen you in ages. How are you?"

It dawned on Tamsin that this was the first time she'd seen Riko and Defne interact. She lifted an eyebrow and sat back to watch.

"Busy, I guess." Riko shrugged but their eyes failed to meet.

From the pile of containers, Defne pulled out rolled vine leaves, cubes of white feta cheese and a grilled eggplant salad.

A thorny silence settled over the courtyard. As the seconds stretched on, Tamsin chewed her lip, scrambling for what to say next. Some hostess she was, two minutes into her own party and the conversation was already stone dead. She opened her mouth but nothing came to mind and she clamped it closed again.

"I've had a good week actually," Defne said and Tamsin exhaled. "I opened my first solo exhibition."

"Nice one." Riko nodded.

"I thought I would feel a sense of accomplishment, you know," Defne said, her voice warming. "But now the bar has been raised, and my current piece is driving me bonkers."

"Tell me about it," Riko mumbled into her beer.

"Sounds like we all need a drink." Defne unpacked a bottle of white wine and two glasses. "Tamsin? Chardonnay?"

"That'd be lovely."

Defne cracked the bottle open and as she handed over a cool glass, the rat in the sink flashed into Tamsin's mind again.

"Shit, Tam. I should've offered you one of my beers," Riko said. Tamsin took a sip of the buttery Chardonnay and waved her away. Riko pulled another brown bottle out of her esky, setting her first empty one aside. "My mum would be horrified. Luckily she doesn't talk to me anymore."

With an awkward smile, Tamsin changed the subject. "Anyone for lamb?" Then without waiting for a reply, she jumped up for the barbecue.

The hotplate was ready. She sprayed it with oil and set her skewers in neat rows. The pink lamb sizzled and the scent of charring meat drifted across the courtyard. Back at the table, Riko and Defne picked at the spread of food. The sputter of fat muffled their conversation, interfering with Tamsin's eavesdropping. The wind shifted and a cloud of smoke from the barbecue blew towards the table.

"Sorry." Tamsin grabbed a tea towel and flapped the cloth, trying to drive away the black smoke. Defne coughed twice, then her eyes went wild and she leaped up to her feet, knocking over her glass of wine. The glass smashed onto the concrete, and Defne—still spluttering—dashed back into the house in a blur of black fabric, almost bowling over Bunty who was hobbling out through the door.

"Defne?" Tamsin took a few steps after her.

Wide-eyed Cecily stepped out of the door after Bunty. "What happened?"

Bunty limped towards the table, her thick walking stick thumping against the hard ground. "Another one of her moods," she said with a dismissive wave. "She'll be back in a minute."

Above their heads, the blind in Defne's window was yanked down hard. Tamsin turned to Riko, who took a nonchalant sip of beer. What happened? Had Riko said something to spook Defne?

"Sarah, this is lovely. Look, flowers," Bunty said.

"It's Tamsin, Grandma," Cecily said in a stage whisper. Then she turned to Tamsin. "Don't take it personally. Sometimes she even forgets mine."

"Oh yes, Tamsin." She reached out and patted Tamsin's forearm. "I feel terrible, we should have done this for you. To welcome you to the building."

"I just wanted to thank you for being so friendly," Tamsin replied.

Cecily plonked a wicker basket onto the table. "Just in case anyone was hungry." She chuckled and unloaded more food. The golden colour was back in her cheeks today. Maybe her illness came and went like the tides.

Tamsin's secret knowledge about Cecily's condition was a heavy weight inside her chest. She avoided meeting Cecily's eye.

"No way!" Cecily said. "The barbecue does work."

"Everyone seems surprised," Tamsin said.

"I'm astounded the landlords haven't taken it away." Bunty eased down onto the bench seat. Cecily served her a glass of the same salmon-pink rose from the previous night and sat down next to her. "About twenty years ago, there was a fire. You can still see the blackened weatherboards on the side of the laundry. Drunken idiots."

Riko drank her beer and stared into space, sitting so still Tamsin had forgotten she was there. Neither Riko nor Bunty had acknowledged each other, and Tamsin braced herself, just in case.

Bunty continued. "I think the barbecue is the one thing our handyman actually maintains."

"I met him yesterday," Tamsin said. "It would have been nice to know he was coming—"

"Strange little man," Bunty said, oblivious to Tamsin's subtle complaint. "Maybe he hopes I'll let men back in one day. And then the barbecue will be ready for them. Fat chance. We don't need those smelly men. Ooh, is that Defne's grilled eggplant?" Bunty leaned across the table and grabbed a forkful, groaning with delight as she slipped it into her mouth.

"The meat!" Tamsin gasped and rushed to her feet.

Cecily ripped the plastic wrap from a bowl of pasta salad, then laid out a baguette. "Riko. Help yourself," she said.

With her back to them, Tamsin held her breath while she turned the skewers, waiting for Riko's retort.

"Cecie makes an excellent pasta salad," Bunty added. "Pesto with artichoke and salami."

"Thank you," Riko replied, without a lick of sarcasm, and Tamsin's shoulders softened. "I haven't had pasta salad in ages."

Tamsin returned to the table and sat down again, this time in Defne's old spot on the bench opposite Riko, facing the back door. She took another small sip of wine, as Riko tucked into

Cecily's pasta salad with an appreciative mumble and Bunty launched into another story from her dancing days.

". . . his beard was dyed, you see. Terribly vain man. And yet he had the gall . . ."

The door opened again and Tamsin's eyes widened.

"Well well well," Cecily said under her breath.

Bunty continued, "so we decided to get the better of him . . . one night . . ." Finally Bunty noticed that no one was listening to her and followed everyone's gaze towards the door.

"Gail!" Bunty leaped from her seat and Cecily lunged out to grab her elbow, stopping the old woman from toppling over. "How lovely to see you."

"The lamb smelt amazing. I had to come down." Gail's normal speaking voice was deeper than Tamsin expected. Full-bodied and well spoken, it had gravitas, a word Tamsin never understood until now.

Dressed in a tangerine linen shirt, Gail sat down on the bench next to Riko. She produced bottles of Tanqueray and tonic from her bag, then a plastic container of ice cubes and lemon wedges. "G and T, anyone?"

Tongue-tied, Tamsin could only shake her head and point to her barely-touched wine.

Riko raised her own bottle. "I'm on the beers," she said with a crooked grin. "I'm Riko, by the way. Flat Two."

"I know," Gail said with the cold eyes of a shark. "I know you all."

The back door opened again.

"Sorry everyone," Defne muttered and skulked back to the last empty seat at the table next to Gail. Then she looked up and flinched at the unfamiliar face beside her.

Tamsin jumped in. "Defne, this is Gail."

"Hello." Defne scrutinised Gail like a museum exhibit.

"Nice to finally meet you, Defne," Gail said in a monotone and stirred her gin with a pink plastic swizzle stick.

Tamsin rubbed her damp palms on her thighs. All six women were at the table, all the residents of Radcliffe in the same place for the first time. The only guest missing was the Voice. She checked the periphery of her hearing, straining for the tell-tale hiss, but there was nothing.

"This pasta salad is so good," Riko said as she helped herself to another serve and Cecily grinned. Close enough in age, they could be friends. If Bunty didn't interfere, of course.

"The meat should be ready," Tamsin announced and then returned with the skewers piled on a platter. "Before we dig in, I'd like to thank you for coming." She picked up her glass and raised it in the air. "To new friends."

"To Radcliffe," Bunty added. Tamsin blinked, Bunty and Radcliffe must be friends again. Then they all charged their drinks in the air, all except Gail who sat back between Riko and Defne with her arms folded.

"Can I take a photo?" Tamsin said.

"No!" Defne and Gail said in unison, and Tamsin recoiled.

"Cecie hates having her photo taken too," Bunty teased and her granddaughter shrugged.

"Okay," Tamsin muttered and lowered her head. "Sorry. I thought it might be nice."

Riko rolled her eyes.

Tamsin cleared her throat and forced herself back into the happy hostess role. "Please, everyone, start eating."

Bowls and platters were passed from one hand to another, plates were piled with salad, meat and bread. Again, everyone except Gail, who rattled the ice in her glass with a thunderous expression.

"So . . ." Gail said once everyone else had started eating. "While we're all here. I have a question . . ."

Tamsin stopped chewing.

". . . which one of you has been going through my mail?"

Tamsin's belly flipped. Confusion clouded over Cecily and Defne's faces, Riko stared down into her plate, and Bunty continued to eat her meal without a care. Perhaps she hadn't heard the question.

"Come on." Gail leaned forward and scrutinised each of the residents around the table one by one. "Fess up. Who's been sticking her nose into my business?"

"Why would I care about your 'business'?" Riko scoffed and prodded at her dinner.

"Riko," Bunty said her name like an insult. "Have some manners, please."

"What?" Riko threw her hands in the air. "She's accusing us of going through her stupid letters and I'm the rude one?"

"It's a simple question. Show a little decorum," Bunty said with a shake of her head. "Unless you have something to hide."

"I'm sure she didn't—" Tamsin tried.

"Me? She's the one who should show some fricking decorum."

Bunty tutted.

"What's your problem with me, old woman?"

"Come on. Don't speak to her like that," Cecily interjected.

"Don't you start." Riko scowled.

Gail slapped the table with her palm. "Someone answer my question!"

"I'll tell you what your problem is," Riko said. "You're racist."

"I'm most certainly not!" Bunty tossed her white head.

"Scared of the yellow peril, eh?"

"Look, I don't care about any of this schoolgirl crap," Gail said. "What I want to know is who's been tampering with my mail?"

"So you're not racist? What is it then?"

"Riko . . ." Cecily reached across the table.

Riko yanked her hand away. "Don't touch me."

Tamsin darted from one angry face to another while Defne mumbled something under her breath.

"I should evict you." Bunty lifted her chin.

"Because I don't sit quietly while someone slags me off? You think you're the fucking Queen of Radcliffe?"

Bunty gasped.

"Don't upset yourself, Grandma." Cecily pressed a hand onto Bunty's skinny arm.

"But you said . . ?" Bunty's brow furrowed.

"Me?" Cecily chuckled. "You're getting confused."

"I'm sure you said . . ." She pressed her ageing fingers against her temples.

Cecily picked up the bottle of rose. "Have a top-up. Let it go. You're spoiling Tamsin's party."

"Come on. Out with it, old woman." Riko's eyes were like lit coals behind her glasses. She stabbed her finger at Bunty diagonally across the table. "What's your problem? Tell me to my face."

Bunty blinked. She set her jaw, then snapped. "You're a harlot! There, I said it. Everyone knows!"

"What?" Riko guffawed. "You think I'm a sex worker? That's it?"

"Don't deny it."

Tamsin frowned as Riko sniggered. Bunty's nostrils flared.

"I could afford somewhere much better to live if I was flogging my arse." Riko shook her head, leaned back and lit up a cigarette. The tobacco crackled as she took a long drag.

"Hey, I'm still eating," Defne grumbled with a mouth full of pasta salad.

"Alright then." Riko threw her hands in the air. "Apparently I'm not welcome here." She stood up and pointed the burning tip of her cigarette at Bunty. "Just so we're clear . . . fuck you. I'm not going anywhere."

"Listen to the way she speaks to me."

Riko scooped up her esky and then turned and jabbed her cigarette in Gail's direction. "And I didn't touch your precious mail." She stormed inside, slamming one door then another.

"Good riddance," Bunty said.

The ground floor window opened and Riko's music blasted into the courtyard. It was familiar, deep whirrs of electronica and strums of a mournful harp. Tamsin held her breath and waited. It was Riko's screaming song.

"She calls that music? Who would pay money for that? Flat number two has always been a problem."

"Satan's work," Defne muttered as she fidgeted with her rings.

Tamsin looked at Defne askance. Black and white images of burnt pig trotters and broken fingernails barged into her head, but no one else reacted to Defne's comment.

"Are you all quite finished?" Gail said. "Because I don't care about any of this. All I want to know is who's been stealing my mail. Cecily . . . Defne?"

"What?" Defne's fork stopped half-way to her mouth as all eyes turned on her.

"Is it you?"

"Me?" Defne's face paled and the skittish, frightened rabbit look returned to her eyes.

"I know all about you. All of you," Gail said. "I'm invisible. I melt through the walls. I see everything you do. You can pretend but I know—"

"If I was you, Gail. I wouldn't come in here, throwing my weight around." Cecily stepped in. "You think you're so innocent?"

"What are you talking about?" Gail narrowed her eyes.

Behind the raised voices, the Voice emerged from the music, and 'Death is coming' blared into the courtyard. Was this the moment? Was this why the Voice had embedded itself in the song? Tamsin sat forward on the bench, hands clutched, knuckles white, scanning from face to face.

"You've had your chance. Looks like I'll have to catch the thief myself." Gail stood up. "You better watch yourselves. I know what you're all up to."

She swept her bottles into her bag and left. The door slammed once again.

No one spoke. The plates were left untouched, Riko's screaming song continued in the background.

"Are we going to get murdered in our beds tonight?" Cecily guffawed.

Tamsin flinched, then covered it up with a feeble laugh. Was Gail the one she should watch?

"She's a little highly strung, that's all," Bunty said.

"Paranoid more like it," Cecily said. "You were a bit mean to Riko, Grandma."

"But . . ." Bunty said, then her face crumpled like a used tissue.

"The heat must be getting to everyone," Tamsin said. "Another drink? Or maybe it's time for dessert."

"You were very quiet, Defne," Cecily said.

"I don't want to get involved." She looked down and poked at the rice salad on her plate.

Cecily eyed her critically and then leaned back with a smirk. "Now I get it."

"This rice salad is delicious," Defne said. "What's in the dressing?"

"It was the smoke, wasn't it?" Cecily continued. "The burning smell."

"What are you on about?" Defne spat. "I've had enough of this." She threw down her fork and struggled up to her feet. "Sorry Tamsin, you tried. But there's no point." She stormed away without collecting her food or her bag, and slammed the door so hard that the glass rattled in the window frame.

"What's wrong with everyone tonight. Is Aunt Flo coming to visit?" Bunty said and raised her empty glass at Cecily. "Where's that top-up, darling?"

Tamsin slumped, staring at the empty seats, angry words still humming in the hot night air. And after all that, there was no sign of the Voice anywhere.

#

Unperturbed by the others, Cecily and Bunty topped up their glasses. They chattered away to each other and tucked into generous wedges of pavlova. Tamsin watched on, taking minuscule bites of the passionfruit, cream and meringue, ensuring that her hands and mouth were busy at all times.

"Aren't people fascinating?" Cecily said, returning to the events of the evening. "If you poke them with a stick, some curl up like snails, and others lash out like cobras."

"Big fuss over nothing if you ask me." Bunty emptied her wine glass then let out a melodramatic yawn. "Excuse me."

"All this excitement worn you out, Grandma?"

"I haven't frowned so much in months. Ungrateful little ... but yes, I think it's time to go upstairs." Bunty hoisted herself up out of her seat while Cecily packed away their things. "Thank you so much for arranging the evening, Tamsin."

"I feel like I should apologise instead," Tamsin mumbled.

"Don't let those hot heads bother you," Bunty said. "I've had worse in the chorus line, believe me."

"I had fun. It was definitely entertaining." Cecily smirked then took her grandmother's arm. They both said their farewells and headed back inside.

Tamsin loitered in the courtyard, not wanting to be alone inside her flat with her failure just yet. What had she done? Rather than help, find the person she was supposed to save, she'd made everything worse.

The music from Riko's flat had stopped and Radcliffe was quiet. She stared up at Riko's and Defne's windows, their blinds now drawn, edges framed with a sliver of light. The evening's disagreements had soaked into the walls, the red brick-work pulsing with bad blood.

#

When Tamsin retreated inside, her flat was stifling. She should have put on her sneakers and headed out for a walk to clear her head, but instead she dumped everything on the floor by her front door and slumped face first into the couch.

What a fool. She should have expected fireworks between Riko and Bunty. Except everyone had behaved until Gail arrived with her gin and paranoia. Maybe it would all blow over after a week or two? But her neighbours didn't strike her as the forgiving kind. And the most disheartening part was that she hadn't managed to uncover a single clue. She sank deeper into the couch, her plan had failed. At this rate, she'd be stuck in this building for months, waiting for a moment which may never come.

Her dress was pasted to her skin with sweat. She dragged herself off the couch and under the shower. The clogged shower head dribbled a pathetic stream of lukewarm water onto her head, and for the hundredth time, she missed her bathroom at home.

Still damp, she lay down in the dark bedroom and stared up at the cracked ceiling, blotchy with water stains. Headlights from a passing car beamed through the flimsy curtains and footsteps pounded above. Gail. The water stains shimmied before her eyes, spreading and darkening like storm clouds. Upstairs. Flat 3. The site of the child murder all those years ago. Did death tarnish everything it touched? Had the homicidal bath water soaked into the wood, the plaster, the paint. Was this why she was here? Did the dead dance behind every door and hide in every corner? Radcliffe was a house death knew well. And a place where it would come again. The only question was when.

Her front door flew open, sending the door handle crashing against the wall. Tamsin bolted upright, terrified. As footsteps stomped across the lounge room, Tamsin scurried out of bed and rushed for the back door. A large black shape loomed in the middle of her lounge room.

"You," the shape growled. A female voice.

Tamsin froze in the kitchen doorway. "Who is it?"

"What do you know?" they hissed.

Tamsin darted for the light switch. As light burst across the room, she gasped, and then frowned. The intruder was Defne. Her dark hair was wild, her eyes huge and gleaming, her lips thick and wet, and she was swinging a wooden club.

"Why are you—" Tamsin said.

Defne thwacked the club against the couch. "Tell me what you know," she growled, raising the club to strike again.

"I—I—I don't know anything," Tamsin said. "Truly."

"Truth? Ha." She slammed the cane into the floor, the thump vibrating across the room.

"Is that Bunty's walking stick? Why do you—?"

"I want to know how you know. Who told you?"

Tamsin shook her head. "I don't know what you mean."

"I thought you were my friend but you've let me down like all the others."

"I am your friend." Tamsin tried to sound calm and sincere, but her voice, and her knees, trembled.

"You know more than you're saying. I'm warning you—don't jump to conclusions."

"Is this about the rat?"

"What?"

"In the sink."

"Don't try to confuse me!" Defne threw the stick down with a clatter.

"Believe me, I—"

Defne lurched forward and Tamsin cringed. Toe-to-toe with Tamsin, Defne stretched up and gripped her shoulder with iron fingers. As her claws dug into Tamsin's flesh, Defne whispered into her ear, her breath hot and garlicky. "Watch your step, liar."

Then without another word, she stomped away, leaving the front door wide open and Tamsin standing there, stunned and shaking.

#

Somehow after Defne's visit, Tamsin managed to sleep. Her dreams were manic and choppy, filled with shouting, spilled wine and dead rats. She heard a voice. Not the Voice but a woman's voice. And it wasn't Defne.

"You heard it. You heard it too. Didn't you?" the woman's voice was clear and piercing. "Wake up!"

Tamsin's eyes flew open. Something rustled in the dark room. She wasn't alone.

"Who's there?" she stuttered, heart thumping inside her chest. Her mind was still foggy with sleep but she was positive she'd locked the door after Defne left.

"Answer me," the woman said again. Whoever she was, she was marching up and down at the foot of Tamsin's bed.

"What do you want?" Tamsin whined.

"Stop fucking about," the woman snapped. "Tell me."

Light from a passing car glinted off a pair of glasses. Tamsin squinted into the dark. "Riko?"

"I know you did," Riko said, her breaths shallow and hoarse. "I know you heard."

"How did you get in here?"

"The death voice." Her head was bowed, her face veiled by dark hair.

"What do you mean?" Tamsin lied.

"Death is coming," Riko mimicked the Voice.

Tamsin simmered with jealousy as Riko repeated the all important words. Just as she feared, the Voice had abandoned her for Riko.

"You heard it too, didn't you?" Riko said.

Tamsin's heartbeat pounded in her ears, her throat tightened. "Yes," she hissed. Then she ripped aside the sheet and leaped from bed, gripping Riko by the upper arms. "Why you?" she screamed into her face.

"Don't touch me!" Riko shoved Tamsin away and she collapsed back onto the mattress like a sandbag. She lay there, panting and blinking as Riko raked her fingernails against her scalp, rambling and unravelling. "It's coming for me. It's what I deserve . . . for what I did . . ."

As Riko paced back and forth, muttering and snivelling, Tamsin's red mist faded. She frowned. What had Riko done?

"How about a glass of water?" Tamsin said, finding a soothing tone. She eased herself up off the bed cautiously. Regardless of what Riko might have done in the past, she was here now to help. "I could do with a drink."

She inched across the room and turned on the light switch. The room flooded with bright light but Riko didn't seem to notice, continuing to pace and mumble. "I thought I could escape. Idiot."

126

Her dark hair was stringy and greasy, she was barefoot, dressed only in a tatty discoloured bra and shorts. Behind her glasses, her eyes were huge and black, skittering from corner to corner.

"Water," Tamsin said then hurried out the door to the kitchen.

She rifled inside the cupboard until she found a reusable plastic coffee cup. No glass for Riko today. She filled it with tepid tap water and delivered it to Riko, who was now standing in the middle of the lounge room.

Riko downed the water in a single gulp. "More," she croaked, and when Tamsin returned from the tap, Riko grabbed the cup and tipped the whole thing over her head. Water streamed down through her hair and trickled over her bare skin.

"Perfect," she sighed. Her eyes stopped their frenetic dance and focused hard on Tamsin's face, absorbing everything like twin black holes. "You know. I know you do. You know exactly what's going on."

Tamsin laughed nervously. "Why does everyone keep saying that?"

"You can't trick me." Riko pointed a finger at her face. "You're not like the others. You're not some sad woman down on your luck."

127

As each day passed at Radcliffe, Tamsin was less sure of the truth. Perhaps she belonged at Radcliffe just as much as the others.

"The voice," Riko said. "The strange voice in my song. You weren't surprised to hear it."

"No, I was." Tamsin pressed her hand against her heart. "Believe me, I was."

"Liar." Riko narrowed her eyes. "I can't stop thinking about it."

"Me too," Tamsin muttered.

"There was enough weird shit in this house before you arrived but then . . . this . . . you brought it with you, didn't you? Why? Why bring it here? To me? Why did you let her find me?"

"Her?"

Thoughts whirled inside Tamsin's head like a blade of a fan. Who did Riko mean? It had been Tamsin's own voice in the song.

"I'm tired." Riko slumped against the wall and slid to the floor. She sprawled on the ground, all elbows and knees and white skin. "So tired. But if I sleep she comes."

"I'll get you more water." Tamsin went to fetch another cup of water but this time she dawdled to the sink, hoping an idea would strike her on the way. Should she call someone? Who? And who had Riko heard in the song?

"Death has come back for me," Riko yelled from the lounge room while Tamsin reached for the tap. "You should be worried too. You heard it. Death is coming for you as well."

Then the front door slammed.

Tamsin rushed back out into the lounge room but Riko was gone.

Chapter Ten

Day Twelve

Her phone rang and Tamsin woke with a groan. Morning had returned and so had the heat, pressing its fiery fingers against the window pane. A headache pounded behind her left eye and all she wanted to do was pull the sheet over her head and disappear forever.

Her phone continued to ring. She rolled over and picked it up. Abby. She grimaced. Despite her threats and her Sunday deadline, she knew her sister wouldn't call the police right away. Should she just answer and ask Abby to come take her home? Forget she ever came here and repair what remained of her other life. It would be cheaper than a taxi but asking her sister for help would weigh on her forever.

Grumbling and indecisive, she let the call go to voicemail. Tomorrow, she promised. Just a few more days. She would prove the Voice she was worthy. She would stop death from coming.

Last night's events churned around in Tamsin's head. Rather than saving a life at Radcliffe, she'd managed to whip five strangers into an angry lather. Defne had accused her of knowing all about something, but what?

Gail kicked it all off by blaming them of stealing her mail.
Although to be fair, Tamsin did have a letter of Gail's in her stash.
Perhaps it was an electricity bill and she'd received a
disconnection notice, otherwise how would she know it was
missing? Gail had said she was invisible and could see through
walls, but she didn't know who took the letters. Or did she? Had
it all been a ploy to make Tamsin confess? Didn't someone
mention that Gail had been a spy? Was Radcliffe riddled with
cameras, as well as ghosts? The letter was unopened. Maybe she
should put it back on the table by the front door and no one
would be the wiser.

Next was Riko with her garbled confession. Like Defne, how
had she got past the locked door? And who had Riko heard on
the tape? Tamsin sighed, a hollow space ached inside her chest.
Had the Voice really left her for Riko? Was she off the hook and
on her own again? But without the Voice, what would Tamsin do
with the rest of her broken life?

Then there was Bunty, with her confused night walks and her
vendetta against Riko. Not to mention Cecily's secret terminal
illness. What kind of soap opera had Tamsin walked into?

Perhaps Bunty was wrong and Radcliffe didn't like Tamsin at
all. In fact, the house hated her and was plotting against her,
creating confusion all around her. Tamsin snorted aloud and
shook her head at her foolish thoughts. What had Cecily called

that condition? Personification? Radcliffe was a building, it didn't scheme and have feelings. Tamsin was being dragged down with the rest of them, into their world of petty problems and delusions.

Tamsin threw on a dress. She hurried out of her flat and knocked on the door to Flat 2, hoping Riko was calmer and more coherent now. After knocking three times, there was no reply.

Back inside her flat, Tamsin scribbled down a note to slip under Riko's door when she spotted Bunty's walking stick lying under the lounge room window, where Defne had dumped it last night. She grabbed the stick and headed up the stairs to the top floor. Yet again her knocks went unanswered and she rested the wooden stick beside the door. Was the whole building empty or just sulking?

Trudging back downstairs, as pearls of perspiration spouted at her hairline and in her elbow creases, a new question unfurled in her mind. How had Defne got hold of Bunty's stick in the middle of the night?

#

Some say it begins once a woman reaches a certain age. The knowledge acquired as she crosses into her crone years, when child-bearing wanes and wisdom blooms in its place. Tamsin didn't know what to believe, but one day she started to hear things. Whispers. Snippets. Words on the wind. After her first encounter at the train station, Tamsin tried to discount the obvious and went to the local hearing aid shop to get her ears tested. An anonymous shopfront in Northland Shopping Centre, a place where no one would recognise, or judge, her. A few bleeps later, Tamsin's hearing was declared fine for her age, although a rabbit-faced woman still tried to flog her a range of ear plugs and ear cleaning sprays she didn't need.

With one door closed, she turned to the cesspit of online misinformation, but what other choice did she have? Everyone knew the old wives tale—hearing voices was a sign of madness. The stigma of mental illness had lessened in recent times, seeking help wasn't going to result in electroshock therapy at an old cold institution. These days, the solution was quick, oval-shaped and taken twice a day with meals.

The more she read, the more she agonised, the more she feared the next time. The Voice was her but it wasn't her. Was it the voice of a different Tamsin? A part of herself she had buried over many years? Or was this someone else inside her head using her voice? A demon? She'd dabbled with an ouija board once, on a high school camp in the bush, but so had everyone else and it was twenty-five years ago. And yet The Exorcist played on repeat inside her mind, all day and all night.

Her sleep became frayed and fitful, she lost all interest in food or even brushing her hair. She found herself eight hours a day in her office, staring at her computer screen as the numbers danced and swirled before her eyes. Her whole world had disappeared into waiting for the next message. Nothing and no-one else mattered. Then her manager, the pocket-sized piggy-eyed Hilary pulled her aside, with a warning about "productivity" and "personal hygiene". Despite all the memos from Human Resources, Hilary hadn't bothered to ask if there was anything wrong in Tamsin's life outside work. If she had, how could Tamsin explain the mesmerising whisper of the Voice to a workaholic like her?

Up until now, Tamsin had been the archetypal good girl, doing as she was told, quietly working away in the corner of life. She squeezed back tears while Hilary gave her a ticking off, but at the end of the working day, she rushed home and fell straight into bed where she spent the whole weekend.

By Monday morning, she'd plastered over the cracks and arrived on the seventh floor of her office building ironed, combed and ready to pretend nothing had happened. Hilary nodded with approval as she clomped past Tamsin's workstation on her four inch heels and Tamsin sighed with relief.

Later that afternoon, she was accompanying Hilary to an important client meeting. Quentin, Hilary's usual wing man for client meetings, was holidaying in Bali.

"Remember you're only here to help answer any technical questions. Only speak if I ask you a direct question," Hilary said before they stepped into the reception area. Tamsin nodded and bowed her head.

Hilary rushed over to a short man in a navy suit standing with his arms folded. He reminded Tamsin of a Staffordshire terrier, with his puffed out chest and stocky arrogance.

"So glad you could make time to see us today," Hilary said as she ushered the client into the boardroom, a hallowed space of shiny wood and high back chairs where lowly tax advisers like Tamsin rarely entered.

Tamsin slid into a chair nearest the door, while Hilary offered him coffee and water. The meeting began with more grovelling and then Hilary opened the presentation folders branded with the logo of Austin & Chow Advisory. While Hilary and the client droned on Tamsin watched leaves dance in the breeze through the floor to ceiling windows.

Without warning, her ears started ringing. "No, not now," she muttered to herself.

The high pitched sting rattled her eardrums and she gripped onto the boardroom table until her knuckles were white.

Hilary glared at her down the table as Tamsin grimaced to hold back the pain.

"Is she alright?" the client asked with a sneer in Tamsin's direction.

Hilary laughed it off. "She's fine. Now this section here on dividends—"

"She looks like she's having a stroke . . ."

"I'm sure she'll be okay." Hilary pointed to a table of figures on the page before them.

The hiss stopped dead, replaced by the sound of rushing blood. Tamsin took a jagged breath and let go of the table. Then the Voice came, insistent and clear in a way it had never been before.

'White car. White man.'

Tamsin frowned and stuck her finger in her ear.

'White car. White man,' the Voice repeated inside her skull. 'White car. White car.'

She glanced up at the client. He was white.

"Do you have a white car?" she interrupted.

The client blinked at her as if seeing her for the first time. He said nothing.

"Yes, I'm talking to you," she said, then repeated "Do you have a white car?" with more intensity.

"Tamsin," Hilary grumbled through a forced smile.

"As a matter of fact I do," he said, glaring at her. "How is that your concern?"

Tamsin faltered under his stare. How could she explain what was happening? The Voice in my head has a message for you? Instead, she stood open-mouthed and awkward.

The client arched his eyebrow at Hilary, and she shook her head. With an eye roll, they turned back to the documents and ignored her.

Red-hot indignation swelled up inside Tamsin and she lurched to her feet. "Listen to me," she yelled.

The client and her manager flinched.

"Don't get into your car," she said. "There is something wrong with it."

Hilary stood up and grabbed Tamsin's arm with manicured nails. "I think you should leave."

"No. He has to listen," Tamsin growled. It's important." She shoved Hilary away hard, too hard. Her manager tripped over her stilettos and toppled to the floor. The client scrambled from his chair to help Hilary up but Tamsin was faster, skirting past Hilary and blocking his path like a netball defender. She stood there, toe-to-toe with the man, and at almost six-foot, Tamsin loomed over him.

"You have to listen to me," she said. "Otherwise something terrible is going to happen. I know it."

For a moment the client's face flickered with fear, but within a heartbeat his natural sneer returned. "You're deranged! Get out of my way." He pushed past her, sending her crashing into the wall.

"You're a fool if you don't listen," Tamsin shouted.

The client helped the red-faced Hilary up to her feet. "Is this acceptable behaviour for staff of Austin & Chow? Violence and rudeness?"

"Of course not. Please accept my apologies." Hilary brown-nosed and dusted herself off. She turned to Tamsin with a scowl. "Tamsin, go back to your desk. Now!"

"No! Not until he listens."

"Alright then." The client folded his fat arms. "What's going to happen? Tell me?"

"I'm saying this for your own good," Tamsin's voice trembled. "Don't get into your car."

"Enough!" Hilary said. "Take your things and go home! We'll talk about this when you've returned to your senses."

"But—"

"Go!"

This time she did as Hilary asked, and ran from the boardroom, fighting back tears. From her desk, she grabbed her handbag and skulked out of the door without a word. Didn't they understand? She'd been trying to help.

On the train home, her hands were still shaking but her head was silent. The Voice was gone.

Tamsin had not been back to Austin & Chow since.

#

The sun pounded down on Tamsin's head as she shuffled shopping bags from one clammy hand to the other. When she turned the corner, glad to see the three-storey Radcliffe in the distance, a couple stood outside the peeling front door. The man, tall and bald, thumped on the door, while the woman who was delicate and dark clutched her hands at her heart.

As she neared Radcliffe's front door, she realised why these people looked so familiar. Her stomach skipped.

"Can I help you?" Tamsin offered with an innocent smile.

The man turned with a frown, his furrowed brow a shelf of suspicion.

"Do you live here?" the woman asked sweetly.

Tamsin jangled her house keys in reply.

"We're looking for someone." The man looked down his nose at Tamsin, even though she was close to his height. "Gail Peterson."

"Does she live here?" the woman chimed in.

Tamsin paused for a beat. "Yes. I don't know if she's home though." Before she knew what she was saying, lies tumbled out of her mouth. "She mentioned a writers conference this morning. I expect she'll be back soon. Do you want to come inside and wait? Get out of this heat?"

"I don't think—" the man started.

"Yes, please," the woman said, and as Tamsin juggled her shopping bags and slid her key into the lock, the man huffed.

They stepped into the dim dusty hallway. The temperature was a trifle cooler inside, but as soon as she stopped moving, Tamsin was flooded with sweat. The couple looked around the foyer without a word but Tamsin knew what they were thinking. She'd thought it herself only ten days earlier.

"Isn't the weather terrible?" she said as she unlocked her flat's door and shoved it open. "I'm just in here." Her heart galloped under her damp shirt. Here was her chance to find out more about the couple, and more importantly, Gail.

"Have you known Gail long?" the woman asked when Tamsin ushered them into her sparse lounge room.

"I've only been here a few weeks but she's been very welcoming. Sorry I don't have air-con."

"At least we're out of the sun," the woman said with a laugh, jittery as a sparrow.

The man said nothing and loitered in the doorway like a storm cloud. He pulled a hankie from his back pocket and wiped the perspiration from his bald head.

"Do you like lemonade?" Tamsin lifted her bags of shopping in the air. "It should still be cold."

"We're fine," the man snapped.

"That would be divine," the woman said. "You're very kind."

"No problem. Any friends of Gail's," she said with a casual shrug. The couple shared a glance and Tamsin pretended not to see it. "Take a seat."

Hurrying into the kitchen, she poured out three glasses. In the background, the bald man hissed at his partner in a staccato. Tamsin wished her hearing was better.

"Here we go." She bustled back into the room with a cheerful grin. The man loomed by the window, silhouetted against the yellowed net curtain and the woman sat on the couch, her knees pressed tight together.

"I forgot to introduce myself. I'm Tamsin." She handed out the drinks, the cold glasses slippery with condensation, and took a seat next to the woman. "How do you know Gail?"

"I'm Lucia and this is Rob," Lucia said. "We used to work together."

"Where was that?"

Rob wrinkled his nose as he looked around the lounge room again. "How long do you think she'll be?"

"I'm not sure," Tamsin replied. "Did you call her before you came?"

"We . . . wanted to surprise her," Lucia said.

"So you were saying you used to work together? Whereabouts?"

"Monash."

"The university? I didn't know Gail was an academic."

"Look. We haven't got all day to hang around," Rob said. "Do you know when she'll be back?"

"Rob!" Lucia scolded. "Sorry, he can be a bit impatient."

He harrumphed. "This is a bloody waste of time."

Tamsin tensed. How could she make them stay? She needed to know more about Gail. "You know, you both look familiar," she blurted. "Have you visited her here before?"

"No," he said, his answer like a slamming door. "Let's go, Lucia."

"We live in the area," the woman added with a nervous smile.

"That explains it. I've probably seen you out on Errol Street. Or in the supermarket. I'm pretty good with faces."

"Come on," Rob grumbled.

"Hold on." She shuffled closer to Tamsin on the couch, then lowered her voice and probed Tamsin's face with her dark eyes. "We haven't seen Gail for ages. How is she?"

Liar.

"Good, I think," Tamsin said with a shrug. "We've only just met."

142

"Has she said anything . . . strange?"

"Ha," Rob barked out a sarcastic laugh.

Tamsin faked a frown. "I don't understand."

"You should steer clear of her," Rob said. "She's unstable."

"Oh." Tamsin blinked. "What makes you say that?"

Lucia gave a tight smile. "We've had a few problems with her."

"What kind of problems?"

"Trying to ram us with her car," Rob said. "Vandalism. Break-ins. We had to get a restraining order. Fat lot of good that's done."

The police at the door. Gail must have breached her court order. More than once.

"Why would she do—?" Tamsin said.

"We came to talk to her." Lucia ignored her question. "Ask her to leave us alone."

Rob folded his arms. "We should have just called the police."

"You said yourself it doesn't do any good, Rob. We have to try something different." Lucia stood up with a sigh. "Sorry, this was a bad idea. We should go."

"Finally," he spat and wrenched open the door.

"Stay. Please," Tamsin floundered. She couldn't let them go so soon. What had they done to make Gail so mad? "I'm sure she won't be much longer."

"Thank you but Rob's right. We should be going."

"If you see her, tell that crazy bitch to leave us alone," Rob said and disappeared out into the hallway.

"No. Don't tell her we came," Lucia said.

"I don't understand. Why would she do something like that?"

"She's not well. Keep an eye out for her. She needs a friend."

Before Tamsin could say anything more, Lucia was gone.

The two doors closed, one after the other, and Tamsin took up Rob's position by the window. She watched as they argued and sniped at each other all the way down the street.

Tamsin's shoulders slumped.

Yet again, all she got was half an answer and ten more questions.

#

The rest of Tamsin's day passed, quiet and uneventful. Defne and Riko were nowhere to be seen, even after the note she'd slipped under Riko's door. After a heatwave dinner of yoghurt and fruit, the oppressive heat sapping her of all energy, she stretched out on the couch to finish Druid's Kiss. When she reached the final chapter, it was past ten o'clock and the traffic outside had died away. As she rushed to the end, the climax between the star-crossed lovers, a scrap of paper toppled out from between the pages and onto her chest. It was torn from an envelope with *14 June 2018 - Fawkner - fire* written in blue biro. Tamsin scuttled upright, staring at the note.

144

Outside her door, someone walked through the foyer and unlocked the front door. Tamsin rushed to the grimy-curtained window and stood in the shadows. Then the footsteps turned back and a cheery knock sounded on her own door. She jumped.

It was Riko with a backpack slung over her shoulder. "I got your note."

"I wanted to . . ." Tamsin clutched onto the door, not quite knowing where to start.

"Want to come for a swim?" Riko asked with a crooked grin.

#

A few minutes later, Riko was leading Tamsin past the panel beater's workshop and into the thick night air.

"The pool's open late because of the hot weather," Riko said. Midnight swim. This explained Riko's wet hair on the night they met.

All the nearby houses had their windows thrust wide open or closed tight with air-conditioners roaring on the walls. Night-owls sat on their front verandahs, drinking and smoking on battered couches, faces uplit by phones.

"I feel like complete shit today. I need this bad," Riko said as they crossed at the traffic lights. "But I only had three beers last night. I must be getting old."

Tamsin was quiet. There was so much she wanted to ask Riko, but where to begin? Her questions were like clumps of peanut butter in her mouth.

The local pool sat on a triangle of land between two roads and the glass entry building was a shining beacon in the darkness. They stepped inside and the blond boy behind the reception desk grinned and welcomed Riko by name.

The outdoor pool area smelled of chlorine and sunscreen. Chill-out house music oozed from the speakers as clusters of young people in their damp bathers sat on the grass, playing cards and laughing. A lone bald man swam laps like a robot while a teenage couple splashed and flirted in the free play lane.

Riko packed away her glasses and slipped off her t-shirt while Tamsin turned away and lifted her dress to reveal her sensible one-piece. Riko in a crop-top and shorts padded across the cement to the pool's edge. A tattoo covered her entire shoulder blade, a black treble clef turning into flying crows. "Hurry up."

Tamsin tiptoed towards the water. "I hope you're not going to swim laps."

"Not tonight." Riko slid into the free play lane and ducked her head under the water.

Tamsin inched down the step ladder and gasped as the cold water enveloped her legs. She pinched her nose and dropped like a stone to the bottom. As she took long languid breaststrokes along the tiled pool floor, all her worries evanesced into the chlorinated water.

When her breath was spent, she resurfaced. She shook her hair like a dog and splattered drops across Riko's face.

"Oi." Riko splashed her back.

"Thank you for inviting me," Tamsin said. "This heat has really been getting to me."

"I know what you mean. I've been coming here every night this week. Swimming helps me think."

Tamsin nodded.

"Until I get distracted by a sound. That's the problem with music, there's nowhere I can completely escape it. It's in the water. The wind. The way people move."

"Maybe in a cave?"

Riko bounced up and down in the water like an energetic child. "How many caves are there around here?"

"True." Tamsin floated on her back and looked up at the bunting strung over the lanes, hoping to find the right way to ask Riko about the Voice in the clear night sky.

"I've been thinking a lot about that song, you know," Riko said. "The screaming song. The one you heard."

Tamsin's heart jolted and she scrambled back onto her feet.

Riko continued. "It's been totally messing with my head ever since. But I think I've worked it out."

"Is that what happened last night?"

"Huh? At the barbecue?"

"Afterwards," Tamsin said.

"What do you mean?" Riko squinted.

Tamsin paused. Was Riko embarrassed? Did she want to pretend last night never happened? In that case, she would play along. For now.

"So, what's your theory about the Voice?" Tamsin almost vomited when she said the word aloud. She wanted to say her Voice but she had to keep a lid on her jealousy.

"You heard of EVP?"

"Is it a band? I'm not very cool."

"Electronic Voice Phenomenon. People have captured unexplained voices on tape ever since recording equipment was invented."

"Voices?" Tamsin gulped.

Riko nodded. "Ghosts."

Tamsin blinked. The idea of ghosts had never crossed her mind. "You think it was a ghost speaking?"

"Have you been to Radcliffe?" Riko scoffed. "It's riddled with weird shit."

"I've heard a few of Bunty's stories," Tamsin said. "Didn't the voice say 'death is coming'? Future tense? A ghost is coming?"

"Time is wibbly-wobbly. Some ghosts are spirits caught in time-loops. The past might be the future to them. Anyway, I know where it came from."

"Yes, you mentioned it last night. It's come for you—"

"What?" Riko snapped. "What are you talking about!"

Tamsin squinted at Riko. Was she acting? Or did Riko really have no recollection of her visit last night? "Can I ask you a question?" she said, choosing her words with care. "Do you ever hear voices in your own head? Like the Voice in the song?"

Riko lifted her chin. Her reply was slow and reluctant. "I hear notes. Tunes. Sometimes my own stupid thoughts, but nothing like that."

Tamsin nodded.

"How about you?" Riko said with a raised eyebrow.

"Yeah, the same," Tamsin replied with a half shrug.

Riko pressed her lips into a thin line and Tamsin's stomach gripped. "Whatever it was," Riko said. "Somehow I captured it. It was real. We both heard it."

"Yes," Tamsin whispered.

"And we don't even know each other. It's not like we fabricated it together."

"I guess not."

"You don't sound convinced."

149

Tamsin chewed on the inside of her cheek. Was now the right time? Should she confess everything? "Do you remember last night?"

"Why do you keep asking me that?" Riko scoffed. "Course I remember. There was a shit barbecue. Although the pasta salad was pretty good. They were all bitches except for you. The end."

"Do you remember coming into my flat? After we all went to bed?"

"What are you talking about?" Riko snapped. "No."

"You said you tried to escape. You mentioned 'her'."

"You don't know anything." Riko's eyes went hard, she clenched her jaw.

"I'm not judging. I want to help. Keep you safe. That's why I've come here . . . to stop death coming for you."

An announcement came over the loudspeakers. "The pool is closing in fifteen minutes."

"We better go," Riko grumbled and pulled herself out of the water. She marched over to their belongings and towelled herself down without another word. When they were dried and dressed, they headed out through the turnstile onto the street again, the air between them as tight as rubber bands.

"You were obviously dreaming," Riko said finally.

"No."

"I think I'd remember breaking into your flat. Don't you?"

"I can't explain it but you were there. Maybe you drank too much. And you said—"

"Look, I don't want to talk about this. I don't know what little fantasies you've got going on but clearly you're the one with the issues."

"Me?"

"Have you ever suffered from delusions?"

Tamsin's eyes narrowed to slits. The Voice was a Gift. She'd been selected and anointed to receive special messages and help others. And now, after abandoning her own home, upsetting her sister and spending ten days in a hot box with a group of odd volatile women, Riko was insulting her?

She clenched her fists and stopped dead. "How dare you!" she roared.

"Whoa." Riko lifted her hands in surrender.

"I am not sick," Tamsin growled.

"Okay." Riko raised her eyebrows and they stomped back to Radcliffe in silence.

Chapter Eleven

Day Thirteen

Since the barbecue, the atmosphere at Radcliffe had been glacial, despite the heat wave. Tamsin found the day's post strewn all over the linoleum in the foyer. She dusted the dirty shoe prints off the envelopes and divided the mail into four neat piles. There were no letters for her of course, no one knew Tamsin was living there.

Glancing over at Riko's closed door, last night's argument gnawed at her. Nonetheless, she was determined to find a way to help Riko, to stop death coming for her. That's why the Voice had brought her here.

A few minutes later, she headed to the courtyard with another basket of dirty washing. In this heat she was sweating through every layer, with more changes than a baby. But there was one advantage to this fiery February, wet clothing dried in no time.

"Fuck!"

Riko's voice echoed across the courtyard as Tamsin opened the door. She dropped her basket and rushed towards Riko, her heart in her throat.

Riko stood in front of a sheet on the Hills Hoist, her hands on her hips, her face thunderous. "It was that racist old bitch, wasn't it?"

The bed sheet was smeared with a large brown stain.

"Is that . . ?"

"Yeah, dog shit. Or maybe it's her own." Riko raised her voice to a shout, her words bouncing off the bricks and concrete. "From her own adult diaper!"

Shit was not Bunty's style, it was far too crude, but this was not the right time to rush to Bunty's defence. "I saw some nappy soaker in the shed," she offered instead.

"I don't need your help." Riko tore the sheet down from the line, pegs popping and clattering to the ground, and stormed inside the weather-beaten laundry shed.

Tamsin slinked back into her own flat, basket in arm. She'd do her washing later. To occupy herself until Riko needed her, she took out a notepad and pen, and started to write. It took five attempts to get it right.

> *I'm sorry if we got off on the wrong foot. I'd like to help you find out who's taking your mail. I'll be home all night.*

> *Tamsin.*

She mounted the stairs and slid the note under the door of Flat 3.

"Are you the one?" said a voice behind her.

Tamsin jolted as she straightened up. "Hi Defne," she replied, her lips twisting into a fake smile.

Defne stood outside her own flat with her arms folded across her bosom and her voluminous black dress. Her dark hair was hanging down straight, thick and lustrous, spun with thin threads of silver.

"Returning her mail after you've read it?"

"Of course not," Tamsin lied.

"Did you break into my flat?"

"Me?" Tamsin recoiled. "It was you who—"

"There are things missing from my flat. Important things. You've been in here, haven't you? Going through my stuff."

"What makes you think . . ?"

"You and Riko. You're in it together, aren't you?"

"I don't know what you're—"

Defne threw something at Tamsin. It bounced off her leg and dropped to the floor. It was a plastic baby doll. The left side of its face was blackened and melted, its cheek sunken and rippled like drips of candlewax.

"Your sorcery won't work," Defne said.

Tamsin picked the doll up between two fingers. "What's this?"

"Don't pretend you don't know. She's trying to make me sick."

"Riko?"

154

"Stop trying to defend her. Stay away from me. Both of you."
Defne spat on the ground and turned away, slamming her door.

#

Glad for a reason to leave Radcliffe, Tamsin walked around the corner to the small neighbourhood bottle shop. By the time she got there, her inner thighs were slick with sweat and chafing. As she stepped inside and was enveloped by air conditioning, she sighed, then headed straight for the gin. She could have picked another brand—one that didn't remind her of her mother—but the familiar green bottle was Gail's favourite too, and everything had to be perfect if she was going to befriend her neighbour.

A quiffed East Asian man stood behind the counter.

"Just this, thanks," she said. Her card bleeped as she tapped it against the reader, and not in a good way.

Card declined.

Tamsin chewed her lip. She'd used her debit card a few hours earlier but hadn't checked her balance. Officially, she was on leave without pay and—until the move to Radcliffe—had been living like a nun from her savings. Money she'd squirrelled away for a deposit on a house of her own. Could she be out of money so soon? Were her entire life savings gone? Opening her empty wallet, she stared at her emergency-only credit card. Wariness of debt was another hand-me-down from her long dead mother, but everything would be back to normal within a few days—she'd leave

Radcliffe behind and sort out her finances. Would Hilary let her go back to her old job after what happened? She flicked away the thought like a pesky fly. Work and money was a worry for another day. Did the client ever take her advice about the white car?

The shop owner was standing, waiting for her, and Tamsin realised she was staring into space. Too polite to say anything, he probably assumed she was another drunk, struggling to find the cash for today's booze. With an embarrassed giggle, she paid and took the gin home to wait for Gail.

#

Halfway home to Radcliffe, Tamsin ran into Cecily. Despite the terrible heat, the young woman somehow managed to look luminous and buoyant. The mere sight of her made Tamsin feel like a saggy stained mattress dumped in the gutter.

Cecily clocked her and waved. "What are you up to?" she said and—after seeing Tamsin's brown paper bag—raised a judgmental eyebrow. "Radcliffe driven you to day drinking already?"

"Oh no," Tamsin spluttered. "It's for—"

"None of my business." Cecily shrugged. "I'm off to get sorbet. Wanna come?"

Tamsin hesitated. What if Gail showed up at her door and she missed her chance? Or if Riko needed her? Sweat trickled between her breasts while she wrestled with her thoughts.

"Watermelon and mint?" Cecily teased.

"That does sound good." Tamsin chewed her lip.

"It's just around the corner."

"Lead the way."

Tamsin and Cecily fell into step together under the punishing sun.

"I haven't seen you since the barbecue," Cecily said.

"What a night." Tamsin rolled her eyes.

"The house has been super tense ever since."

"Tell me about it."

"Maybe it's the heat."

"Maybe." Tamsin paused. How much should she say?

"Defne's been even stranger than usual and I heard Riko yelling earlier."

Before Tamsin knew it, she was telling Cecily the story of Riko and Defne's bizarre midnight visits. It felt good to tell someone else.

"How did they get in?" Cecily asked.

"That's what I want to know. Now I'm really worried about Riko." Tamsin stopped short before she mentioned the Voice. One strange story at a time. "Then today Defne was accusing Riko . . ."

"Wait a sec. I'm getting confused about who's angry with who. What's Riko done to Defne?"

"Some kind of witchcraft, apparently. She thinks Riko left a doll in her flat. A baby doll with a burned face."

Cecily frowned. "Sounds like one of Defne's art pieces."

Tamsin chewed on her lip as they turned the corner. "You're right. It does."

Up ahead, the tiny sorbet shop was surrounded by groups of hipsters on milk crates licking pink, yellow and pale green sorbet.

"Lucky," Cecily said as they stood in line behind an older couple with arty thick framed glasses. The handwritten menu on the wall had three flavours crossed out. "They've still got watermelon."

"I would have thrown a tantrum if they'd sold out." Tamsin smirked.

Cecily chuckled, then let out a deep sigh. "Seriously Tamsin, what are we going to do about the house?"

"What does Bunty say?"

"I can't talk to her about Riko. She's got this idea fixed in her head that she's some kind of Satan worshipping hooker trying to corrupt us all. She can be so old-fashioned."

The line moved briskly and Tamsin was soon licking fresh minty sorbet from a miniature wooden shovel. Two of the milk crates were free and they sat down to eat.

"Did Bunty say anything about the others?"

"She doesn't see a problem. Then again, she does come from dancing, which must have been one hell of a bitchy business." Cecily licked at her mango cup. "And I reckon she's seen far worse in the house. It's not like anyone has died. This time."

A high pitched laugh burst from Tamsin's mouth. She blushed, cleared her throat and changed the subject. "How's uni going?"

Cecily launched into a lengthy explanation about an assignment on social identity and someone named Zimbardo. As Cecily prattled on, Tamsin's pink sorbet melted to slush. She lifted the paper cup and poured the sweet cold sauce into her mouth.

"Thanks for dragging me along. It was perfect." Tamsin stood up and wandered over to toss her empty cup into the bin. When she turned back, Cecily was on her feet, swaying like a sapling in a strong breeze.

Tamsin rushed forward and caught her by the elbow. "Sit down," she ordered and the pale-faced Cecily obeyed without question. Tamsin hurried to the counter for a glass of water.

With trembling hands, Cecily took the paper cup from Tamsin and sipped slowly. "Sorry," she muttered. "It must be the heat."

Tamsin squinted at her. "Have you taken your medication?"

"I don't have a choice," she said with a weak smile. "Wait a sec. How do you know? Of course, my bag."

"Is it serious?" Tamsin winced. There was no tactful way of asking the question.

Cecily shrugged.

"I'm sorry."

She shrugged again. "Let's go home."

"Are you up to the walk?" Tamsin asked, concern heavy in her voice.

"Don't fuss. I hate it when people fuss. And I'd prefer it if you didn't tell anyone else."

Tamsin crossed her heart. "Absolutely."

Cecily stood up again, this time on steady legs, and they ambled back to Radcliffe through the thick heat.

All the way home, three words were on Tamsin's tongue.

Death is coming.

#

14 June 2018 - Fawkner - fire.

Tamsin stared at the scrap of paper in her fingers, the note which had fallen out of the pages of Druid's Kiss. She pulled out her phone and tapped in the same words. Her search returned results from the Herald Sun, The Age and ABC websites. She chose the top story.

Five die in Fawkner house fire.

Two adults and three children perished in a house fire in Fawkner last night. Authorities believe the fire was started by faulty wiring.

Tamsin poked her tongue into her cheek. Why would Bunty leave a note about a fire inside a book? Did she know the victims? Or had she lent the book to someone else before Tamsin?

A fist thumped on Tamsin's door. She jumped.

"Open up!" they shouted.

She flinched and shoved the note into her handbag, then scampered to the front door on tip-toes.

"I know you're there!"

She recognised the voice. Gail must have seen her note, but this was not the neighbourly visit she'd intended. She inched the door open to Gail's flushed face. Her eyes were narrowed to slits.

"Why are you here?" she snapped.

"Sorry?" Tamsin blinked.

"I saw you with them. You're working for them, aren't you? Spying on me."

"The police?" Tamsin said with wide innocent eyes. "They left a note, I think."

"Not the police! Was that you as well? I should have known. You're a troublemaker. Everyone here kept to themselves until you came along," she spat, stale gin on her breath.

"Me? I'm only trying to—"

"It all makes sense now, you're the one who's been going through my mail. Reporting back to them on my movements. Are you a private detective? No. You're an amateur through and through." She jabbed a finger into Tamsin's face. "You let them in here. Into my home. Did you tell them where I lived?"

Tamsin stood bewildered in her own doorway. She gnawed on her lip.

"They won't win you know. I'm cleverer than they are. They should know that by now. And you should know it too."

"You mean the couple who visited yesterday? Rob and Lucy, was it?"

Gail scoffed. "Scum."

"I found them standing on the doorstep. It was stinking hot out there. They told me they were friends of yours. They seemed nice, so I let them inside to wait for you."

Gail clenched her jaw and inspected Tamsin with surgical precision. Tamsin's pulse thumped in her neck as she tried to keep her face calm.

"Hmm," Gail grumbled. "They would do that, especially her."

"I'm sorry I let them in. I didn't know. My mother always said I was too trusting."

"What did they tell you?"

"Do you want to come in?"

Tamsin waved her inside, and with a grumble, Gail nodded and stepped into the lounge. Tamsin was buzzing as she raced over to clear the clean washing off the couch. This was her chance to speak with Gail one on one. Beside the couch, the copy of Druid's Kiss was lying on the floor. It was almost too perfect, like a prop in a play. It must be fate.

Gail brightened when she spotted her own book.

"Bunty lent it to me," Tamsin said. "I don't usually read romance but I was absolutely hooked. I finished it last night."

"Thank you," Gail said, this time in a quiet and genuine tone.

"Can I offer you a drink? It must be time for a G and T?"

"My favourite."

"I remember. Make yourself at home. I'll be back in a sec."

In the kitchen, Tamsin cringed. Did her comment about gin make her sound attentive, or just plain creepy? Like a stalker.

"Sorry, I don't have any ice," she said, returning with the drinks and handing one to Gail.

"Thank you," Gail said, and before Tamsin had a chance to say cheers, she took a long slurp. "Tell me. What did they say about me?"

"Not much," Tamsin said. "Rob, was it? He seemed a bit grumpy and, if I'm honest, quite rude."

"He's a thieving bastard!"

"Were you involved? Romantically?"

163

"No!" Gail spat and then started to laugh. "Heaven forbid."

"Lucia seemed nicer—"

"Don't be fooled."

"She said you used to work together."

"That's where it all began."

Tamsin leaned back into the old couch and sipped the sweet and sour drink, the juniper tickling on her tongue. She waited, letting the silence linger, hoping Gail would fill the gap and tell her everything. The quiet stretched on until it became painful. Tamsin gripped her glass tight and bit her lip. Patience, she reminded herself.

"Bunty told me I'd have peace here," Gail said, her voice burdened. "I need quiet to work. I can't have them interfering. Not again. They've taken everything from me. I won't let them take this too."

"What happened?" Tamsin wriggled closer. "If you don't mind me asking."

"It's no secret. They stole from me. Stole everything. And no one believed me. They still don't believe me. Those two made everyone think I was crazy. That's their power. Conniving cunts."

Tamsin flinched. "Money can bring out the worst in people," she consoled.

"If only it was money." Gail huffed. "Money comes and goes. It was worse, much worse. They stole my soul."

Tamsin's mouth dropped open.

On the other side of the room, Tamsin's phone rang from inside her handbag. "Go on," she said to Gail. "I'll let it go to voicemail."

Gail raised an eyebrow and Tamsin goaded her with a nod. The phone trilled in the background and as soon as it stopped, it started to ring again.

"I'm so sorry." Tamsin hurried over to her bag and fished out her phone. It was Abby. She switched the ringer to silent and glimpsed a message from her sister.

I've called the police.

With a sigh, Tamsin shoved the phone back into the depths of her bag. "Sorry about that," she said and sat down again. "Go on. Please."

Gail took a sip of gin and continued. "At one time, we were all friends. We worked together in the History Department. Colleagues working together towards the same aims," she spat out a bitter laugh. "Or so I thought. Idiot. Rob and I did our undergrad together, side by side, pushing each other in playful competition. Lucia came later. She became Rob's girlfriend. I thought the three of us were a team. But I was wrong."

Tamsin gave a sympathetic nod.

"They took it all from me. Years of research. Thousands of hours of reading and thinking. I was obsessed, I can see that now. Towards the end of my PhD, I barely slept or ate. Living in the faculty building or the library. And just when my masterpiece was done, they ripped it from my hands and claimed it as their own."

A tomato-red rash spread up Gail's neck. "They denied it, of course. They said I'd been working too hard. That I was having a breakdown. They had the audacity to claim I hadn't even finished my dissertation. It wasn't true! But no one believed me. They twisted everything I said and turned everyone against me. Manipulative bastards."

She sniffed and tossed her head. "I went to the Dean. She was wary at first and tried to talk me out of it. Suggested counselling instead. I'd always suspected she preferred Rob over me. But I know universities take plagiarism very seriously. They need to. So despite their efforts to shut me up and make me go away, I bypassed the Dean and made a formal complaint. There was an investigation. A panel of senior people from across the University. I got my day in court."

Tamsin leaned forward.

"But Rob and Lucia got to them too. My claim was thrown out. Lack of evidence. Rubbish!" She scoffed. "I was slapped on the wrist for making egregious claims and told to go back to my research like a child. Pricks."

"How awful."

"I will never let them forget what they did to me. I wait six months. Or a year. And just when they think it's all over and I've moved on, I reappear and fuck with them." Her face took on a devilish gleam. "Rub their thievery and lies in their faces all over again."

Tamsin nodded. With eggs and strawberry milkshakes.

"So you see why I am so wary," Gail went on, and the wicked spark faded away. "At least I have my books. They can't take those away from me. I'm sure they look down their snobby noses at romance anyway." She sighed. "Speaking of which, I should get back to them."

Gail stood up and drained the rest of her glass.

"Oh." Tamsin tried to hide her disappointment with a smile. "I guess books don't write themselves. I'm really looking forward to reading the next one."

"I'll bring you a copy of my latest. Hearts of Stone and Moss."

"I'd like that."

"Thanks for the drink. I'll see myself out."

Before Tamsin could argue, the door had closed and Gail was gone.

The truth about Gail was nothing like the outlandish stories the others had concocted about her. And yet, more tragic. Gail's footsteps thumped on the ceiling above her head. The sound of a woman broken by betrayal.

Then Tamsin remembered. Abby.

#

"I just forgot to call you," Tamsin said, her sister answering after two short rings. "You didn't have to go to the police."

"You didn't think I meant what I said? You know me better than that. I'm worried about you. Where the hell are you?"

"I told you. I'm down at Torquay."

"I thought you said you were in a hotel in the city?"

Tamsin grimaced. She was losing track of all her lies. "I decided to go down the coast instead," she bumbled. "Sea change?" She laughed unconvincingly at her own joke.

"And how is the holiday?" Abby spat. "Nice and restful while I'm here worrying about you all night?"

"I didn't ask you to . . ." Tamsin stopped. She took a couple of calming breaths and soothed her tone. "My room is just a few streets back from the beach. Nice and quiet. Most of the tourists have gone home."

Abby grumbled. "So when are you coming home then?"

"Did you really call the police?"

"Answer the bloody question, Tam."

"I think I'll stay a couple more days. What day is it now?" She laughed again. "See how relaxed I am."

There was silence and Tamsin squeezed her eyes shut. How could she make her sister understand she was fine?

In the end, Abby was the one who spoke. "Are you taking your meds?"

"Yes," Tamsin murmured.

"Bullshit."

"I feel better."

"No. No. No. We talked about this. You can't just take yourself off. You need medical supervision. I know you didn't go to Dr Prasad."

"Are you checking up on me?"

"Someone has to. Look at you. You're falling apart. You've lost your job. You've gone wandering off somewhere. You're telling lies."

Tamsin clenched her jaw.

Abby continued. "Just come home. Alright?"

"You don't understand," Tamsin blurted.

"Explain it to me then."

"I need to be here. There is something I need to do."

"What's so important?"

"I have to save someone's life."

"What? Tam?"

"Seriously. The Voice . . ."

"This is exactly what I mean. You're hearing fucking voices! You need to start taking your medication again."

"It's not about me. I need to save someone. It'll be over soon and then I'll be back."

"No, Tam," Abby said with a sniffle.

Was her sister crying? Her tough lawyer no-nonsense sister?

"Please. Don't worry about me. I'm fine. Really."

"But I do. There's only you left."

"Soon. Just a few more days," Tamsin said. "I knew you'd understand if I explained."

Abby coughed, clearing the emotion from her throat. "Listen. If you won't look after yourself, someone's going to have to do it for you."

"What do you mean?"

"Come back tonight and it'll all go away."

"You can't do that!"

"I've found a place for you. It's for your own—"

"You won't find me, you know. Neither will the police."

"Tam—"

Tamsin threw her phone across the room. She slumped forward and hung her head in her hands. Abby wasn't serious, was she?

Chapter Twelve

Day Fourteen

Another sticky night passed and the air inside the flat was a thick suffocating casserole. That morning Tamsin was putting away her cutlery and cursing the heat when she found it. Sitting on top of the forks and spoons was a small toy mouse, grey with tatty pink ears and button eyes. She plucked the mouse out of the drawer by the ear and inspected it between two fingers.

Another rodent in her kitchen? She threw it across the room and out the kitchen door, sending the mouse skidding and rolling over the lounge room floorboards. Was it Defne again? Or someone else? The child's plush toy was nowhere near as disgusting as the shit on Riko's sheets, but someone was still poking fun at her.

"Who are you?" she said aloud. "And what the hell are you up to?"

There was a knock on the door. She jumped. Hopefully it was the odd handyman, back to fix the sash window in her bedroom. What she wouldn't give for a tiny gust of fresh air through the flat.

"Hello," Riko said in a small voice as Tamsin opened the door.

Tamsin gave a little gasp. Then composed herself and beamed. "Hi."

"Can I come in?" Riko said, her head bowed, looking up through a curtain of dark hair.

"Of course."

Tamsin stepped aside to let Riko in, and as she passed, she checked Riko up and down. Aside from a smudgy shadow under her eyes, she appeared in good health. Death hadn't come for her, yet.

"Look . . ." Riko started. "About the other night . . ."

Tamsin sat down on her old couch and patted the cushion beside her. "Sit."

Riko shook her head but closed the front door.

"I'm glad you've come," Tamsin said. "I've been wanting to talk to you."

"Let me go first. Please." Riko leaned against the wall. "I'm shithouse at this type of thing but I have to grow up sometime."

"I'm all ears," Tamsin clutched her hands in her lap.

Riko sighed. "Firstly, I didn't mean to be such a bitch. But I swear I never came into your flat."

Tamsin said nothing.

"You've obviously got your own problems. Hey, who doesn't? But I didn't need to treat you like . . . wait a sec. What the fuck!"

Riko stomped across the room and snatched the toy mouse up off the floor. She cradled it against her chest. "How the fuck did you get this?"

"I found it," Tamsin said in a small voice.

Riko's eyes blazed behind her glasses. "This is mine. You've been inside my flat."

"No, I haven't. I can't explain how . . . but it was in my kitchen . . ."

She yelped. A harsh hiss swelled inside her ears and she clutched at the side of her head. Nausea scorched inside her belly, burning a pathway all the way up to her mouth.

"Not now," she grunted.

"What are you saying to me?" Riko spat.

The screech in her ears turned deafening. Swarms of floaters in red and purple clouded her vision.

"Are you okay?" Riko's words were muffled, as though her question was travelling through water.

Tamsin moved her mouth to reply but her thoughts were interrupted by a familiar refrain.

'Death is coming.'

The three words rang in her head and Tamsin repeated it like a mantra. She rose up from the couch, onto her feet. "Death is coming."

"No. Stop," Riko croaked. "Why are you saying that?"

"Death is coming," Tamsin chanted, a duet with the echoing voice inside her head.

"Shut up!" Riko howled.

"Death is coming."

With the words still fresh on her lips, all her strength drained from her body. She collapsed like a discarded marionette and everything went black.

#

Sometime later, she roused to find Riko standing over her with a damp cloth in her hand.

"What the fuck was that?" Riko said.

Tamsin squinted and rubbed her aching neck. "The Voice."

"What voice?"

"The voice from your song. It lives in my head."

"Huh?"

"This is what I've been wanting to talk to you about."

"Your head?" Riko frowned. "Then how did it get into my recording? It sounded like . . . ."

"I have no idea."

Riko's face went white as milk, her eyes wide and magnified behind her glasses. "It's coming for me," she whispered. "Isn't it?"

With a groan, Tamsin grabbed the arm of the couch and hoisted herself upright. "I can't be sure. The Voice led me here to help someone. Maybe it was you."

"This is fucking nuts."

"I know . . ."

"Weird voices from your head turning up in my song?" Riko raked her fingers through her hair. "In *her* voice?"

"Who's voice? Who did you hear?"

"I can't think. This place is so hot, it's like a sauna. I don't know how you can live like this." Riko flung open the flat's front door, then paused in the doorway. "You coming? I've got a fan."

Tamsin hurried after Riko with a tiny smile. Her head was still pounding, yet her heart felt huge in her chest. Were the pieces finally coming together?

#

Inside Riko's flat, a pedestal fan blew air over Tamsin's clammy skin. She sat on the squishy couch with Riko beside her, rolling a joint from a small pottery bowl.

"Death has been after me for eight years now," Riko said. "Ever since the night I killed my twin sister."

Tamsin's breath tripped inside her throat. Murder? Is that why the Voice brought her here?

Riko licked the joint closed and lit up. "I didn't kill her with my own hands. But it was my fault. And my family won't let me forget it. And neither should they." Smoke streamed out of her open mouth, the white fog masking her eyes.

Riko offered Tamsin the joint. Tamsin shook her head and Riko continued. "That's why I'm here in this shitty place, all alone, making my twisted fucking music. I'm in hiding. Hiding from a vengeful demon, but it's come for me."

She stared down at the carpet and cleared her throat. "I'm the worst sister imaginable. I betrayed my own twin. Her name was Hina."

A thousand thoughts zipped through Tamsin's head. She tried to keep her face impassive, sympathetic, while hurrying to stitch everything together.

"I was a selfish bitch. Always have been. Hina had something I wanted and I couldn't just be happy for her. I had to ruin it, didn't I? So I took it from her. I took everything from her. We should have gotten old together. Me and her. I always thought we'd be the type of twins who died within minutes of each other."

She reached for an ashtray.

"His name was . . . it doesn't even matter . . . I still can't believe I betrayed my sister for some dickhead. He should have been the one to die!"

Tamsin pressed her lips together.

"Anyway, it was my fault. She came home and found us in bed together. She went apeshit. Angrier than I've ever seen her before. Smashing perfume bottles and chairs. Then she stormed out and got into her car. I shouldn't have let her get behind the wheel. I should have fucking stopped her. Twice I failed her. I seduced him and then I let her drive."

Riko curled her shoulders, her voice shaking as she continued in a whisper. "Her car hit a tree. They said she'd been going at a hundred and sixty. Bang. Hina, my twin, my only sister, my best friend. Gone."

Tamsin leaned over and brushed Riko's arm. She flinched and Tamsin pulled her hand away. Riko took another long mournful drag.

"My family found out what happened. All of it. Hina wasn't even cold when they threw me out of the house. I wasn't allowed to go to the funeral. Apparently sluts weren't invited."

"That's terrible," Tamsin said.

"I went to her grave on my own. I knew she didn't want me there. She's still angry with me. You see, our mother is from Osaka, and our bedtime stories were Japanese folktales. We always liked the gory ones. Both of us. Especially the ones about vengeful ghosts. Onryo."

"And you heard your sister in the song?" Tamsin frowned.

"She's been trying to get back at me for years. I've evaded her so far. She's just found another way to let me know she's after me."

Tamsin chewed her lip as she tried to follow the logic. "Then why have I heard it too?"

"You're clairvoyant or something, aren't you? You've channelled her or whatever it's called. You must know more about this stuff than me."

"I'm an auditory psychic. I hear a Voice."

"So you only hear stuff? I didn't know that was a thing."

"Neither did I until recently. The message brought me here to Radcliffe to help someone."

"Ah. So that's why you freaked out about the screams?"

Tamsin nodded. "I've been sent to watch over you and make sure it doesn't happen."

"How are you going to do that? Death is inevitable. Have you got magical powers as well?"

Tamsin's stomach clenched. How could she stop death? She hadn't thought through the final, most important, part of her plan.

"We'll think of something," she said, pasting on a smile. "I'm right next door. Just thump on the wall and I can be over here in a flash."

"What if we listen to the song again? Together. Maybe it'll give us a hint of what to do."

Before Tamsin could reply, Riko scampered over to the desk covered with monitors. A chill scurried over Tamsin's skin as she braced herself to hear the Voice again. Her jealousy had faded but now she felt lost and untethered. The reason she was here was clear, but what should she do next?

The now familiar song started, whooshes followed by the thump of bass and then the sombre harp. Tamsin scrunched her hands together until her fingers turned bright red. While she steeled herself for the Voice, she'd forgotten about the screams. And when the first shriek sounded, she yelped and clamped her hands over her ears.

The music stopped and Tamsin dropped her hands.

Riko was standing by her computer. "It's not there."

"Sorry?"

"The voice." Riko tapped at the keyboard. "I'll play it again."

She replayed the track. Whirring, whooshing, thumping. Harps. Screams.

Riko lifted a finger in the air. "Now. It should come in now. Listen. Nothing. It's gone. How can it be gone?"

Tamsin rubbed the back of her neck. "I don't understand?"

"Neither do I. It was there and now it's not."

Tamsin's mind whirred like a carousel.

"Does this mean she's gone?" Riko asked, her face shining. "Did you fix it? Has she forgiven me?"

"I'm not sure," Tamsin said. A tight band of confusion squeezed at her chest.

"Thank you," Riko sniffed.

Tamsin replied with a pained smile, then scrubbed her hand across her forehead. What the hell was going on? None of it made any sense. Why did the Voice appear then disappear from Riko's song? She exhaled. Was Riko right, had Tamsin stopped death from coming? Or did it mean nothing, and she was back to square one?

#

Tamsin was slurping on a slice of watermelon when someone thumped on the Radcliffe front door. Her belly tightened. She tip-toed to the window and peered out of the grimy curtains. Two figures in blue uniform were at the door, and a police van was parked across the road. They knocked again and she held her breath, listening for movement in the other flats. She suspected they were home but no one came out to answer the door.

After the third unanswered knock, the police gave up and drove away, and Tamsin slumped against the wall. Maybe she wasn't the reason they were visiting Radcliffe, perhaps Rob had complained about Gail again. She pinched the skin at her throat. Or was her first instinct correct and Abby's threats weren't empty after all?

Her phone bleeped and Tamsin flipped it over, pulse quickening as she swiped through and opened the message. It was an email from the Angel Listener. At last.

This is quite a dilemma, dear Tamsin.

I consulted with my own guides on your question and they were unanimous in their response.

Tamsin exhaled and licked her lips as she read on.

You must cleanse yourself. Fast, meditate and spend three days in solid prayer. The channel is clogged and needs to repair. Your mind must also be cleared, the messages are getting confused . . .

Tamsin clicked her tongue and put the phone down without reading to the end. Her shoulders sagged. This was not the answer she needed. Just as she feared, no one knew how to help her. She was all on her own.

#

Sleepless yet again, it was after midnight when Tamsin retreated to the courtyard where at least there was a breeze. She set herself up on the battered picnic table and glanced up at the darkened windows of Flats 2, 4 and 5. Riko, Defne, Bunty and of course Cecily.

A pen in her hand, she jotted down her thoughts and theories, tearing a hole in the paper as she tried to piece everything together. But how could she find logic in the illogical?

Cecily was ill and possibly terminal. This meant death could be coming for her soon, but with no medical or nursing skills, what could Tamsin do? Friendship and comfort was all she could offer. Was this enough? She rolled this idea around in her mouth like a boiled sweet, then shook her head.

Bunty, as lithe as a fairy one day and hobbling with a stick the next, already had death on her doorstep. Nothing could stop nature's course and the prediction from the Voice felt more unexpected and brutal.

She turned her attention to Riko. While the Voice had disappeared from her song and Riko now thought she'd been absolved, a dark cloud still hovered over her. Her dead sister, her estranged family, her guilt and self-loathing, all made Riko a definite candidate. Tamsin tapped her pen on her lip and a plan sprouted. A way she could help. A warm tingle danced through her body as she wrote down her ideas.

Next was Defne. With her mood swings and dark disturbing art, she was friends with the macabre. Tamsin grimaced. Was her behaviour all part of a performance? Then again, Defne's life had been scarred with heartbreak and betrayal. Was she harbouring a hunger for revenge? And there was another unanswered question, from Defne's break-in after the barbeque, what terrible secret did she think Tamsin knew?

And then there was Gail, her anger still as hot and destructive as lava. Lucia's warning rang in Tamsin's ears. Could she trust anything that Gail said? Or after their evening of gin and candidness, was she officially on Team Gail now?

And what about the rat, the toy mouse, the doll and the shit on Riko's sheets? Tamsin clenched her jaw. How did it all connect? She couldn't sit and wait much longer for the answer to appear. If the police were looking for her, they'd be back again soon.

Above her head, the tin roof creaked, shifting and fidgeting in the warm night air. There was someone Tamsin was forgetting, someone who had been there from the very first moment. Radcliffe, the house itself. Could death be coming for Radcliffe?

#

A box was sitting outside Tamsin's door when she returned from the courtyard. Her stomach churned as she inched towards it. All the unpleasant surprises of the last few days flicked through her mind again. With her breath held, she flipped open the lid. The box was filled with various paperback books, all written by LG McGovern. It was Gail's entire back catalogue. Tamsin exhaled and picked up the note sitting on top of the pile.

I've found somewhere else quiet to write. I hope you enjoy these.

Goodbye.

Gail.

With a sigh, Tamsin dragged the box inside her flat. She lay on the couch and stared up at the silent ceiling. Flat 3 was now vacant. Did this mean she had one less person to worry about?

Returning to the box, she pulled out the first book. The title was Memento Mori. Tamsin squeezed her eyes shut.

Remember you will die.

Chapter Thirteen

Day Fifteen

The next morning, Tamsin heard footsteps on the stairs and poked her head out, hoping to catch Defne. She had to convince Defne she had nothing to do with the charred doll, which was now sitting with Tamsin's other Radcliffe keepsakes. But when she opened her door, the footsteps were elegant, a dancer's. It was Bunty, and Tamsin frowned as the old lady skipped down the last few steps.

"Any mail for me?" she asked, sashaying across the linoleum. "If no one has stolen them."

"I saw some for Cecily," Tamsin said. "How is she by the way?"

She fixed on Bunty and waited for a shadow of sadness to cross her face, but the old lady walked right by her and picked up her granddaughter's stack of mail.

"She's such a delightful creature. I'm so lucky to have her," Bunty said.

Tamsin blinked. Was Bunty putting on a brave face? Dancers were like actors, weren't they? Professional liars. Or could Tamsin be the only one who knew Cecily's secret?

"It's such a shame about Gail leaving us, isn't it?" Bunty said. "Radcliffe and I loved having such a talented writer under our roof. Then again, people come and they go."

Tamsin chewed her lip and nodded.

"And how are you, Tamsin?" Bunty continued. "Any more rats?"

"No. Nothing."

"That's good. We don't want to drive you away too, now, do we?" Before Tamsin could reply, Bunty was halfway up the first flight of stairs. "Toodle-ooh," she called over her shoulder with a finger wave.

Watching the old woman climb the stairs, Tamsin stood outside her open door. A frown spread as her mind swirled, and as answers formed and fell into place, her jaw slowly dropped.

"Of course," she said and chuckled to herself.

#

In the city, the sun was ricocheting off the concrete and glass, the heat intensifying and stifling. Outside an office building, Tamsin tried to shelter under the shade of a half-dead tree. She'd left Radcliffe looking respectable but the air-con in the tram was broken, and now she was a mess of sweat and straggly hair. The heat always peaked after five o'clock in Melbourne, as though the sun worked a dull office job and raced out of the door as soon as the clocks struck five.

All day, Tamsin had poured over Linkedin and Facebook, stitching together the life story of the man. A Certified Practicing Accountant with thirty odd years experience, a keen bushwalker, an avid Blues supporter. Thanks to social media and Google Maps, Tamsin managed to pin-point where he worked. She tingled with a cocktail of excitement and anxiety, and hoped the man didn't work long hours.

The revolving door spewed office workers out into the sun, tearing lanyards from their necks and loosening their ties. While she waited, searching for the one particular face, she invented her own guessing game. As each person stepped out into the ferocious heat of the afternoon, would they smile or would they groan?

After another ten minutes, she jolted to attention as a man emerged from the door. A little greyer than the photograph on LinkedIn but she was positive it was him. Perhaps ninety percent sure.

She lunged from her spot by the withered tree towards him. He didn't notice her at all, his head probably swimming with stresses from the day, or what to eat for dinner.

"Excuse me," she said.

He kept walking.

She rushed closer to him. "Sorry."

He glanced up with a look of disdain.

She smiled her most genuine smile. "Are you Daniel Royle?"

"Yes." He stopped and frowned.

"Do you have a daughter called Riko?"

He recoiled. "What do you want?"

"I know where she is."

His eyes widened. "Where?"

#

After a trip to Little Bourke Street and a dinner of dumplings swimming in chilli oil, Tamsin headed back to Radcliffe. Itching to share her theory on who was behind the trouble in the house, she knocked on Riko's door but there was no reply. Had her father charged straight to the house to apologise, and whisked her away? Tamsin had no way to check, in the brief time they'd known each other, she and Riko hadn't exchanged numbers. In fact, she hadn't shared numbers with anyone in the building. When this was all over, she would leave Radcliffe without a trace that she was ever there.

Tamsin went upstairs, and butterflies wrestled in her belly as she lifted her fist to knock on Defne's door. Her ears buzzed with static and a burp of bile scurried up her throat. A single word, delivered by a familiar Voice, drifted in.

'Warm.'

Her lips curled into a smile and she rapped on the wood with confidence.

"What do you want?" Defne answered the door in another black baggy dress.

"I just wanted to . . ."

"Apologise?" She raised a dark eyebrow.

"I can explain! The doll didn't come from Riko. Or me."

Defne pursed her lips into a bloodless line and pushed her door closed.

"Wait!" Tamsin grabbed the edge and wrenched it back open. "Come with me upstairs."

"I'm not going anywhere." Defne yanked at the door but Tamsin held on until her knuckles were white. "Let go!"

"Listen. It was her all along. I don't know why. Maybe she enjoyed the game."

"Who?"

"She can go anywhere." Then a mess of non sequiturs tumbled out of Tamsin's mouth. "You said other things had gone missing, right? It all makes sense. The building master key."

"Gail?" Defne squinted.

"No, not Gail."

"She said she knew everything about us."

"It's not her. Come upstairs," Tamsin urged. "We'll confront her together."

"Cecily?"

Tamsin shook her head.

"Bunty?" Defne sneered. "No way."

"I think she misses the drama of the stage. And now we're her puppets and she's leading us in some weird and twisted dance."

Defne chewed on her lip and let go of the door. "You think she's the one who's been snooping around my flat?"

Tamsin nodded. "Around all our flats."

"I've had nightmares about that doll." Defne fussed with the silver rings on her hand. "Was it supposed to be a joke?"

"And I didn't get a chance to tell you about the rat she left in my sink."

"Rat?" She blinked.

Tamsin cleared her throat. "I have to admit, I thought it was you at first."

"Me?" Defne baulked.

"Your art?" Tamsin said with an apologetic shrug. "My guess is she planted it there to come between us."

"What do you mean?"

"She didn't want us to be friends."

With blank eyes, Defne stared in Tamsin's direction but looked straight through her. Seconds ticked by in silence and Tamsin waited, her hands and jaw clenched.

Defne's rigid shoulders and hard expression softened like dough. "I thought you'd stopped liking me," she said.

"Not at all."

Defne scrubbed her hand through her hair. She tapped her sandalled foot on the floor, slow at first. The slapping of the sole against the floorboards gradually sped up into a frenetic beat. Her neighbour gritted her teeth and Tamsin could almost hear the thoughts clashing inside her head.

"Jealous old cow," Defne spat, her words like fireworks. "She won't get away with this." She pushed past Tamsin and stomped across the landing to the staircase. Tamsin followed, and at the top of the stairs, they found the door to Flat 5 ajar.

"Hello," Tamsin called and pushed it open. In the middle of the lounge room Cecily stood facing the door with her arms folded and a bemused expression.

Defne barged past Tamsin into the flat. "Where's your Grandma?"

"We'd like to speak to her," Tamsin added.

"Really?" Cecily cocked an eyebrow. "What could that be about?"

"Don't play games. Bunty! Get out here now!" Defne bellowed and Tamsin flinched at the force of her voice. Cecily guffawed behind her hand.

"What's so funny?" Defne blasted.

Cecily lifted her hands in surrender.

"What's all this racket?" Bunty appeared in the doorway, dressed in a floral nightie with her cane in her hand. "Oh it's you, Defne. Is something wrong?"

Defne's anger was like a desert wind as she glowered at the old woman hobbling across the room, each step accompanied by the thump of her walking stick. Tamsin's belly roiled as Bunty drew closer. Something was wrong. She switched her focus back to Cecily, a wicked gleam in the young woman's eyes.

"Wait." Tamsin placed a hand on Defne's arm.

"What?" Defne lurched at Tamsin's touch.

Cecily smirked. "Why wait?"

"What's going on?" Bunty said, arriving at Cecily's side. "Why all this shouting?"

Before Defne could reply, Tamsin jumped in. Another piece had fallen into place. "I was wrong. It wasn't Bunty after all."

#

"Of course it wasn't Bunty," Cecily said. "It was me."

Tamsin inhaled sharply and beside her, Defne flared her nostrils like a horse.

"I borrowed her skeleton key," Cecily continued. "And opened all your doors. I snuck around. Taking things. Leaving little presents. And leading trails to other people. It was all me."

"Why?" Tamsin squeaked.

Cecily ignored her. "And the shit on the sheet. That was me too. Defne, did you like the LSD in the pasta salad? Was it fun?"

"You little bitch," Defne grumbled.

"Do you smell burning, Defne?"

"Shut your face," Defne said, jabbing her finger into the air.

"I know everything. What do you reckon? Should I tell them?" Cecily stepped forward with a smirk. "Or should I call the cops instead?"

"You're not so squeaky clean yourself."

"Oh really?"

"You're not who you say you are," Defne said.

"Ha. And who is?" Cecily said. "These walls are papered with lies. I know. I've been through all your things."

Bunty hobbled up to Cecily's side. "That's enough, Cecie," she scolded. "You're upsetting everyone."

"Oh, shut up!" Cecily spun around. "Go to bed, you old bag."

Bunty reeled back a step, blinking at her granddaughter.

"Hey," Tamsin said. "Don't talk to your grandmother that way."

Cecily turned to Tamsin. "Mind your own business. Who are you, anyway?"

"What do you mean?" Tamsin stuttered.

"You've been snooping around ever since you moved in. I opened every one of your cupboards, every drawer. I found all the trophies you'd stolen from us."

"Trophies?" Defne's lips curled in disgust.

Tamsin swallowed. Luckily she'd hidden her notebook in the vegetable crisper. Imagine if Cecily had found the notes she'd written about all of them.

"I don't know what you're talking about."

"But I still don't understand . . ." Cecily said. "Why are you here, Tamsin? If that is your real name."

"Course it is," Tamsin said. "I just needed somewhere to live. There's no big mystery."

"You expect me to believe that?" Cecily laughed. "Does anyone here have the guts to tell the truth?"

"This is completely bonkers. I'm out of here," Defne said, then pointed at Cecily. "You stay away from my flat. Okay?"

"I'll do you a deal, Defne. You confess your sins and I'll never go near your flat again."

With a growl in her throat, Defne turned and stormed away.

"Defne," Tamsin called after her. Her sandals thwacked across the landing and down the stairs.

"Oh well. Maybe I'll go first." Cecily preened her hair. "Defne was right about me, and it all started with Bunty over here."

Her grandmother's face was vacant, humming to herself as she swept her arms through the air, running through her ballet arm positions. Was Bunty even listening?

"When I saw her in the supermarket I knew she was the one. The perfect target."

Tamsin's mouth fell open. She turned back to Bunty, who had her arms in a circle above her head.

"That's right." Cecily grinned, walking over and giving Bunty a patronising pat on the shoulder. "Sorry to break it to you but I'm not your granddaughter. In fact I'm a complete stranger. No relation at all."

The pale Bunty said nothing, her graceful arms gliding through the air to a silent symphony.

"What kind of monster are you?" Tamsin cried.

Cecily shrugged, then bent down and spoke to the old woman like a child. "I'm sorry I lied, Bunty. I'm not your long-lost daughter's child. I didn't track you down through your dancing accolades. It was all made-up. We don't share the same blood. We're just one more of Radcliffe's lies."

Bunty's eyelids fluttered and her arms dropped to her sides. "Perhaps it is time for bed."

"Do it yourself." Cecily rolled her eyes. "I've had enough of being your nurse. I've had enough of this place and all of you." She waved her arm. "Radcliffe was supposed to be my little personal lab, a group of single lonely weird women I could experiment on. Reading the literature about Leary and Janov and Spring Grove wasn't enough. There are still boundaries to be pushed and nothing beats first-hand experience. You and the others were the ideal guinea pigs, with only your neuroses and dark pasts to keep you company. But the results were totally pathetic—just a lot of shouting and sulking. You were supposed to kickstart my stellar career as a psychologist. I needed something revolutionary but you gave me nothing. Useless—the whole lot of you. Even Bunty and her obsession with this stupid house is old news." She sighed. "Oh well. Sometimes we have to admit our defeats. Fail fast, don't they say? Time to pack up and try again somewhere else."

Tamsin tugged at her collar as her head swam, not knowing what to say or do next.

"When I first saw Bunty in the canned soup aisle," Cecily rattled on. "She looked perfect. So arrogant and self obsessed with her pretentious hand gestures, still pretending to be a ballerina after all these years."

"How can you be so cruel?" Tamsin interrupted.

"You think this is cruel? Ha. Do you want to hear my sob story?" Cecily leered.

Tamsin cringed in anticipation.

"It's not what you think." Cecily held up a hand. "Daddy was a doctor and mother was a painter. Respectable and completely self-absorbed. Totally devoted to their careers and oblivious to their little daughter. I didn't starve but I was making my own dinner from five years old from whatever I could find in the pantry. No one molested me and I had somewhere to sleep, but they acted as if I was invisible." Cecily lifted her chin high, but despite her defiant posture, her voice shook.

"I'm sorry to hear that," Tamsin said. "It sounds awful . . . but why are you here tormenting an old lady, a stranger, rather than your own parents?"

"Bastards died in a car crash when I was eleven. Good riddance."

"Missed your chance to get them to notice you?" Tamsin muttered to herself, low enough to escape Cecily's ears.

Bunty pressed her age-spotted hand over her face. "I'm tired, Cecie."

"Piss off. I'm done with you." Cecily flicked her hand dismissively.

Tamsin bustled over to Bunty. "I'll help you. Which room is yours?"

She pointed with a shaking hand towards the doorway and Tamsin held the crook of her elbow as they exited the room, leaving the smug Cecily behind.

#

Bunty said very little as Tamsin helped her into her single bed. Tamsin kept quiet too, not knowing what to say, imagining Bunty's shattered heart under her nightie. She pulled the sheets over her and Bunty rolled towards the wall, then Tamsin slipped away, leaving the bedroom door ajar.

With a deep breath, Tamsin steeled herself in anticipation of another run-in with Cecily. But then a black blur swooped up the hallway towards her and she flinched. It was Defne.

"You scared me." Tamsin pressed her hand against her throat. "You're back?"

"Where's Cecily?" Defne said. All her earlier fury was gone, and was now as calm as marble.

"I'm not sure," Tamsin replied, plastering on a smile as her pulse quickened. She'd never seen Defne so composed before.

"I know she told you," Defne said.

"Told me what?"

"Everything."

"I don't—" Tamsin stumbled.

Sweat glistened on Defne's upper lip as a mist fell over her eyes. "It all started when I found them. In my bed. Our bed. Eighteen years I'd given that bastard. I knew he wasn't perfect— who is—but what kind of person rubs it in your face like that?"

Tamsin took a step back, pressing herself against the wall.

"And with her. We'd both known her, Ayla, since our Saturday Turkish classes at the community centre. She was ugly back then, buck-toothed and pizza-faced. Flat as a boy. I had the curves all the boys wanted in those days." She smirked. "Sevkat was short but he was a man, a real man, even when we were teenagers. You know how some boys stay boys? Not Sev."

Tamsin found herself nodding.

"We were never blessed with children. Turns out it was my fault. Once he kicked me out, and Ayla moved in, she soon got pregnant. She already had three of her own. She was a widow. Her husband got crushed by a reversing truck at work."

Tamsin grimaced.

"You have to understand, I did nothing wrong. I was the victim." Defne tapped her chest. "I smiled at mosque. At birthdays and weddings and funerals. I knew what they were all saying about me. I was the barren one, the bad wife, sent back home to her parents. Returned goods destined to look after them until they died because I was good for nothing else. He cheated on me but I was the outcast. I became the ghost they all ignored. How can that be fair?"

Tamsin shook her head. "It's not."

"And he forgot all about me. Like I never existed. He should have changed the locks. I chose a cold night. All it took was a few switched wires. A jammed lock and a gas leak. I learned a thing or two from my old dad. Sev didn't know his arse from his elbow. And her? Ha."

She stopped and let out a deep sigh. "Usually on Friday nights, the kids went to their grandparents. The fire spread so quickly. And hot, so hot. Like a furnace."

Tamsin stiffened. Fire? The note inside Druid's Kiss?

"I'd planned to be miles away when it happened. Booked a ticket to Noosa and everything. In the end I couldn't go, I needed to be there. To see his face. I wanted him to know it was me. But I did a better job than I expected. The only one who survived was the little three-year-old boy. Poor thing."

Tamsin's eyes bulged. "You killed a . . ." She smothered the rest of the words behind her hand.

Defne's face crumpled. She rotated the three silver rings on her hand, one after another. "For months, I waited for the police to knock on my door. Arrest me for murder! Or at least question me. But no one remembered me. I wasn't even worth considering as a suspect. I even went to the funerals but surprise, surprise, they all ignored me again."

"You went to the funeral?"

"To make sure the bastard and his slut were dead. And because it was expected. No one cared. No one said 'we're sorry for your loss, Defne.' There was no sympathy for me. His widow.

It was all about what a wonderful man he was. Ha. I don't regret a single second."

"Except for the children," Tamsin whispered.

Defne nodded with a pained smile. Then she lifted her gaze and stared straight into Tamsin's eyes, as though seeing her for the very first time. Somewhere inside a switch flicked. "She didn't tell you, did she?" Defne's tone was as cold as steel.

Tamsin froze. "Um . . ."

"You didn't know." She stepped forward, so close Tamsin could smell her vinegary breath. "I made a grave mistake."

"I won't say anything."

"Of course you will," she scoffed. "Like you could keep this to yourself."

"Seriously. You can trust me. I've got my own secrets."

"Nothing as big as this, I'll bet. This will eat away at you. I killed children. A baby and two little girls."

Tamsin placed a shaking hand on her heart. "I promise you."

"There's one way I can be sure."

"Name it."

With a wicked laugh, Defne produced Bunty's walking stick and smashed Tamsin across the temple. Wood met bone with a flash of agonising pain and then everything went black.

#

Tamsin's skull was bumping along the floorboards when she woke up. Defne had her by the leg and was dragging her towards a door.

Tamsin grabbed for her temple and her fingers came away slick with blood. "Stop," she cried, flailing her arms, grabbing for the walls, trying to wedge herself in the doorway.

Without a word, Defne stopped. She dropped her grip on Tamsin's leg and smashed a heel into her belly. Tamsin yelped and curled up into a ball, then Defne shoved her into through the door like a bundle of dirty washing.

"What's going on?" Cecily called, from somewhere deeper inside the flat.

"Help," Tamsin moaned.

"You!" Defne yelled back over her shoulder. "This is all your fault!" In a whoosh of black fabric, she slammed the bedroom door shut, trapping Tamsin inside.

Tamsin rubbed her head and pressed at her bruised ribs with a wince. With no bones broken, she hoisted herself up to her feet. Getting her bearings, she glanced around the room. She was back in Bunty's small bedroom and Bunty was tucked up in the single bed where Tamsin had left her.

A shrill discordant whistle blasted in Tamsin's ear. She tasted vomit.

'Screaming,' the Voice said. 'Screaming.'

"Defne!" Tamsin hurried to the door and reached out for the handle, but there was nothing there. "What the . . ."

"She took it away," Bunty said matter-of-factly.

Tamsin searched the door up and down, looking for a way to open it from the inside but it was closed tight. She bashed her fists on the wood. "Open the door! Defne?"

"It's no use," Bunty said but Tamsin kept thumping. "She's in one of her moods. She won't listen."

Outside the door, someone screamed. Tamsin unclenched and rubbed her sore hands. Was it Cecily or Defne screaming?

Cecily had somehow unravelled Defne's secret. All those digs about fires and smoke now made sense. And of course, the doll, too.

Tamsin glanced around the small spartan room. Bed. Bedside table. Lamp. She sighed. Nothing she could use to force open a door. She turned to Bunty. "Where's your phone?"

Bunty lay like a mannequin under the sheets, staring up at the ceiling.

"Bunty . . . phone?"

She waved weakly towards the door. "Out there somewhere."

Tamsin rushed to the large window overlooking the street. It was closed. She wrapped her fingers around the small metal lifts and heaved. The window didn't budge, and on closer inspection, it was painted shut. Cecily again?

Tamsin wilted. She rested her forehead on the tepid glass. Pregnant charcoal-grey clouds swarmed over the afternoon sun. Rain was coming.

Tamsin left the window and slumped on the ground alongside Bunty's bed. "I can't believe it was Cecily. The rat. The shit on the sheet. The break-ins."

"It was all of them . . . feeding off each other," Bunty said. "No one is innocent here."

"You are. Cecily tricked you. You seem so calm."

"Radcliffe will look after me."

Tamsin frowned. The house again. Then again Radcliffe had probably been Bunty's only friend for many years. Until Cecily came along. Cecily the liar.

"But you took her into your home. Treated her like your own grandchild. I'd be so angry if I was you."

"Radcliffe knows everything. All about beginnings and endings. Nothing is an accident here. That's why you moved in. Why you were drawn here."

Tamsin blinked in disbelief. Unlike Bunty, she knew it wasn't Radcliffe inside her head.

There was a thump, somewhere on the other side of the door. Then a fresh scream. Cecily?

A sly smile spread over Bunty's face. "I'm the last person who should hold a grudge, as these walls know."

"You've forgiven her?"

"There's nothing to forgive. I knew all along. From the moment we met, I knew she was not my grandchild."

Tamsin's eyes widened.

"I played along with her games. Then it all became very confusing. Apparently I started to sleepwalk and she said I needed to be locked in here at night. For my own protection. To be honest, I didn't mind. Here with my friend Radcliffe, I'm never alone." Bunty rolled over and stroked the wall. "Radcliffe listened to my troubles like she'd always done. This was just the latest chapter in my story and we all know stories must eventually end."

"Some days I would watch Cecily across the room and wonder why. Why was she here? Why was she pretending to be my granddaughter? I have no money. The best she could get from me was a roof over her head and a meal or two. Now I understand. She needed me in her own twisted way."

"How did you know?"

"It was impossible. She can't be my granddaughter. My baby died."

Tamsin gasped. "I'm so sorry."

Their relationship now made a kind of twisted sense. The grief over a lost baby would be endless and Bunty—in her twilight years—must have been pining for a grandchild, then along comes

Cecily with her lies. Unhealthy but convenient, they latched onto one another, playing out each other's fantasies.

"The crying. He would never be quiet. Day and night. Week after week. Relentless."

Tamsin's heart froze in her chest.

"Never sleeping, never letting me sleep. I couldn't take it anymore. I didn't have anyone to help me. No one could know I had a child. A single mother even in the seventies was a terrible sin. And I received my punishment, my child was a demon. It wasn't even mine, I'm sure of it. Radcliffe took care of me. I owe Radcliffe everything. She told me what to do. A bath. A quick way to end the crying. Then it was so quiet. So peaceful."

She smiled.

#

Thump. Thump. Thump.

Someone was banging against the door.

Tamsin scrubbed her palm over her forehead. How many murderers lived in Radcliffe? She was starting to lose count.

Thump. Thump.

The slow rhythmic thud tore her away from Bunty's confession. She hurried over and in desperation placed her mouth over the tiny crack between the door and the jamb. "Let us out," she called into the gap.

The thumping continued.

"Please, Defne."

"This is the only way," Defne said from the opposite side.

Tamsin slapped her hand against the wood. "Come on, Defne. Open the door."

"You can't ignore me," Defne said and continued to slowly pound on the door. "I am not invisible."

Tamsin leaned her cheek against the paint. "Where's Cecily?"

"She doesn't matter."

"I heard screaming. Is she okay?"

"Why do you care about her?"

"Open the door. We could talk. I could help you."

"Ha," Defne spat. "You?"

"I thought we were friends."

On the other side of the door, something was shuffling. Tamsin broke into a grin and scurried back, making room for the door to open.

A high pitch noise screeched in her left ear.

'Warm.'

Tamsin clutched her head as the walls swirled and bile burned up the back of her throat.

'Death is coming,' it whispered.

"I know," she snapped back. "I'm trying to stop it."

'Death is coming.'

The door stayed closed. Footsteps thumped away.

"Defne!" Tamsin dropped down onto her belly, flat on the floor. "I can help you," she yelled through the gap under the door. "Please. Just let us out."

'Death is coming,' the Voice said. 'Warmer.'

"You're not helping," Tamsin hissed.

"Can you smell smoke?" Bunty asked from the bed.

Tamsin's eyes widened as she sniffed the air. Thin trails of smoke were seeping under the door.

"No!" Tamsin scrambled upright and shouldered the door as hard as she could. She cried out in pain as her bones and joints shuddered against solid wood. The door barely flexed. Smoke streamed into the room, scratching at her nostrils and throat.

"Defne!" she croaked.

Slow footsteps approached the door. "I told you this was the end," Defne said through the wood. "Death is inevitable."

"No. No. No. It doesn't have to be! Open the door and we can sort it out." Tamsin turned to Bunty. "Are there smoke alarms in Radcliffe?"

The old woman shrugged and coughed into her hand. Tamsin raked her fingers through her hair. Gail. She stamped her feet on the floor hard. Surely Gail would hear them and come up to complain. Then she remembered Gail was gone. And with Riko out too, there was no one else home to help.

'Death is coming.'

"Shut up," Tamsin screeched. "Give me something helpful."

"Don't yell at me," Bunty said with a wheeze.

"My secret is going to die with me," Defne shouted through the door.

Tamsin scoured the smoky room again. A small bedside table and a lamp. She turned to Bunty and handed her a pillow. "Lay on the ground, and put this over your mouth."

"Radcliffe won't be happy about this," Bunty grumbled as she slipped out of bed.

"None of us are."

Further away, deeper inside the house, something smashed into the wall. The bang followed by a piercing desperate scream.

"Cecily?" Tamsin gulped. She grabbed the bedside table, sending the lamp smashing to the floor, and slammed it into the small window. The pane shattered and cool air rushed inside. The southerly wind had finally arrived. A mineral scent whipped into the room, the salty perfume of the first drops of rain.

She looked down. It was ten metres to the pavement below, with nothing to soften a fall but a white car.

'Death is coming.'

Tamsin's head whirred, her throat and lungs were raw. Bunty was curled up in the corner, the pillow clutched to her face. A broken leg or hip was better than dying in a fire, but not even the petite Bunty would fit through the window. Let alone her with her six-foot frame.

The room was hazy, and the smoke stung her eyes. Defne was again rhythmically thumping at the door and humming.

Tamsin touched the door. The wood was warm. The fire was coming and Defne was waiting.

'Hot,' said the Voice inside her head. 'Hot.'

Hysterical laughter sliced through the air. Defne's laughter.

'Death is coming,' the Voice repeated as Defne's cackling turned into a hacking cough.

Tears dribbled down Tamsin's face as her head throbbed and smoke filled the room. She picked up the bedside table again and with gritted teeth, slammed the pine frame into the door. The bedside table smashed apart, but the door stayed locked tight and Bunty's underwear spilled across the room. With a trembling lip, Tamsin tossed aside the broken wood and slid down the wall.

Slumped on the ground, she clawed at her throat, blind and fighting for breath. A muffled cough came from the corner.

"Bunty?" Tamsin croaked. She dragged herself along the floor in the direction of the old lady. She could still save someone. But her arms and legs were as weak as noodles.

On the other side of the door, Defne screamed.

"Bunty, I'm here," Tamsin rasped as she struggled towards her, her muscles screeching in pain. Then halfway across the room, she stalled like a car without petrol, every last drop of strength and fight had drained from her body, and she collapsed.

'Death is coming,' the voice insisted.

"I tried. I tried." Tamsin lay face down and sobbed into the wooden floorboards. "I believed you." Then with a choked whimper. "I never realised you meant . . ."

'Boiling.'

Flames roared behind the door and a clap of thunder shook the windows and walls.

Death was here.

MADELEINE D'ESTE

Acknowledgements

Radcliffe was inspired by my love for gothic fiction in combination with an idea about an auditory psychic who heard the words 'death is coming'. Thank you to all the writers of gothic fiction from Anne Radcliffe herself to the "modern" writers like Silvia Moreno Garcia, Susan Hill and Kate Morton for your wonderful tales of high drama in spooky houses.

There are many people I need to thank who helped to shape Radcliffe along the way. Jon Black and the New Moon Critique Group for their encouraging and thought-provoking critiques, as well as the Melbourne Writers Group – Claire Bright, Tonia Schuster, Ste O'Connor, Jake Knight and Mark Philips.

Thank you to the team at Deadset Press for taking on this little book about a weird building filled with weird women. I also have to thank the Twitter Monthly Challenge crew, and Kristy Acevedo. The Monthly Challenge provides accountability and discipline, as well as a fun supportive group of emerging writers. Thank you for helping me through the bleak seemingly pointless writing days.

And lastly thank you to Melbourne, to her architecture, her weather and her landmarks in North Melbourne, Kensington, West Melbourne and Albert Park, for inspiring the streets where Radcliffe sits. As well as Radcliffe herself.

And thank you to my friends and family for your understanding when I squirrel myself away to make up stories.

About the Author

Growing up in Tasmania, Madeleine D'Este now lives in inner-city Melbourne surrounded by books. After studying law (and never practising) and travelling the world, Madeleine now lives a double life, immersed in the corporate world by day and writing female-led speculative and mystery fiction by night. Madeleine hosts the weekly Dark Mysteries book review radio show/podcast on artdistrict-radio.com, as well as Write Through The Roof, the podcast for writers.

When not writing, Madeleine enjoys podcasts, knitting, forteana, indie films, kettle bells and likes her coffee as 'black as midnight on a moonless night'.

About the Author

ABOUT DEADSET PRESS

Deadset Press is an independent publisher of incredible speculative fiction. We provide publishing pathways for emerging writers from Australia and New Zealand, and aspire to shine the light on unique and diverse voices.
You can learn more at:

www.deadsetpress.com

ALSO BY DEADSET PRESS